# A FAR CRY

### Lost Xentu
### ~ Book 2 ~

## MARIE JUDSON

A FAR CRY
Copyright © 2023 by Marie Judson

Published December 2023
Indies United Publishing House, LLC

Cover art design by Tatiana Villa
Formatting by The Book Khaleesi

*First Edition*

ISBN: 978-1-64456-670-1 [paperback]
ISBN: 978-1-64456-671-8 [Mobi]
ISBN: 978-1-64456-672-5 [ePub]
ISBN: 978-1-64456-673-2 [Audiobook]

Library of Congress Control Number: 2023947679

INDIES UNITED PUBLISHING HOUSE, LLC
P.O. BOX 3071
QUINCY, IL 62305-3071

# OTHER BOOKS by MARIE JUDSON

**Braided Dimensions Series**

Braided Dimensions: Book 1
Stretched Across Time: Book 2
Strange Alliances: Book 3
Pasts Undone: Book 4

**Lost Xentu Series**

Elf Stone of the Neyna: Book 1

# Part I

# CHAPTER

# 1

**Y**anda lay on her childhood bed, gazing through tears at her nearly one year old, half-elf son. "What are we going to do, Zami?"

Zami was nothing if not precocious. He blinked at her, trying to suss out what she needed from her thoughts, his whirling elven eyes studying her, seeing more than most could.

She pushed up on one elbow and gazed with a sad smile into his face. "I wanted to introduce you to your sister."

"Sister. Seiti," he said.

"Yes." They held a picture of her in their shared mind. It was from when she was six, nearly two years ago. She would look different now at eight.

Yanda listened for her adoptive parents. They would come to her room soon. At least Omshi, the only mother she'd known, would. Yanda, thirty-six in Alland years, was by profession a surgeon, but she'd just returned from

Terlond, a planet where she'd been held captive for over a year.

"Yanda?" Omshi called from the hallway. "Please come out here and speak with me and your father. You at least owe us that much. Some sort of explanation."

Yanda pushed to standing and held out her arms to Zami. She swooped him up, twirling him, kissing his neck. He chortled. "We won't be here long," she whispered in his ear.

"We find Seiti." He spoke with assurance.

Yanda nibbled his ear. Her son's ability to talk with such maturity never failed to amaze her. She assumed it was due to the mind communication since even before he was born. Not just with her but with his Elven father, away in the Forest of Rotoul. She suggested quietly, "Glam your ears and eyes?" Much as she hated to ask it, she knew his reception in this world would be better if he showed no exo-signs. In fact, it could save his life.

His face crinkled with amusement, and like it was a game, he turned away, then back to her. No leaf-shaped ears, no whirling irises.

"That's very good," she said, throat tightening. *Not for long, not for long*, she chanted to herself.

\* \* \*

"Who's this fine fellow?" Nedri set his pipe aside and opened his arms.

Yanda set Zami down. He was beginning to walk, if holding a finger.

"Come help with dinner," Omshi said from the doorway, watching their progress with crossed arms and creased brow.

Yanda's adoptive father pulled the boy onto his lap.

Zami solemnly examined the man who held him.

"So, what do you have to say for yourself?" Omshi handed Yanda a stack of plates.

Yanda set the table. Omshi brought dishes into the dining room from the kitchen.

"I didn't leave without word on purpose." Yanda took glasses from a shelf. "I was abducted."

Omshi turned to her, hand on hip, eyes narrowed. "Abducted. By whom?"

As if she doubts me, Yanda thought. Does she really think I ran off on purpose? "It's a long story. I can tell you over dinner." Yanda collected utensils from a drawer lined with shelf paper, a familiar task from her childhood.

"Your daughter cried every night." Omshi ladled stew into bowls.

"I cried for her, too."

"You should. You're her mother."

"Can't you have sympathy for me?" Yanda stopped laying knives, forks, and spoons. "I was abducted. Can't you ask, 'Did you suffer?'" Pressing her lips in a line, Yanda forced herself to stop. She and her adoptive mother had always gone at it. It did no good to talk to her mother like that. It only made things worse.

Omshi shook her head as she set a platter of meat on the table, followed by overcooked vegetables.

Nedri appeared in the doorway holding Zami. "Something smells good." He was the peacemaker though he seldom took action in family affairs. That was Omshi's domain.

Yanda brought a stack of cloth napkins and started setting them with the utensils around the table. It had been nearly two years since she'd done such a thing. "Any new projects?"

Nedri returned to his chair, still holding Zami who did not protest. "I always have something going. You know that."

Yanda kissed the top of his balding head. He quirked a smile.

"I think I still have your high chair," Omshi said. "In the garage."

Yanda went to find it. The small garage, off the kitchen, had Nedri's work bench, and shelves neatly labeled. The high chair, paint-worn, stood to one side among furniture awaiting repair or give away. She lifted it, then noticed a box labeled "Seiti". Already they'd boxed her things? An old *evaporator*—converting waste to organic matter or air—bobbled its domed plaz lid as she pushed past and opened the box. Baby clothes, too small for Zami. What she needed was recent: notes, drawings, photos, anything that might give her a clue as to where Seiti went, who she might have met. She carried in the high chair.

Omshi said her blessing learned at the Church of Vital Promise, while Yanda thought her own silent prayer to find her daughter.

"All are welcome in our folds. Preserve their Way, Almighty Bright One, and light our paths toward goodness."

It sounded kind and healthy, but they were bigots, Yanda thought. They did not welcome everyone.

Omshi served herself a slice of meat and nodded for them to do the same.

Not being a meat-eater, Yanda put *patat* and limp *sadi snip* on her plate. She gave Zami the same.

"The boy might want meat." Omshi held out the platter.

"As you might recall, I don't eat meat," Yanda said, tasting the overcooked parsnip-like root, imagining it lightly sauteed in olive oil and garlic. "Neither does his father. When Zami gets older, if he wishes, he can choose to eat meat."

"His father...that man who brought you here?" Omshi eyed her with unfeigned disapproval. Tenali showed no signs of his Elven half but he wore the clothing of an unaffiliated space pilot, his hair long and unruly, covering his ears.

"No." Yanda did not add, "Zami is Tenali's uncle." One step at a time. "They're related, though. Tenali just brought me home. He's..." What was he to her? How could she sum up all they'd been through? Truth be told, she didn't much want to, seeing Omshi's pinched expression. "He's a friend. And has a ship."

Nedri cleared his throat. "You've got mail from the hospital."

"I bet I do," Yanda said, though she didn't know why it would come here and not to her apartment in the city. Her account was on auto-pay. She'd need to check on that, and go to the hospital, to see if she still had a job.

"It's on the *cabra* in the hall," Nedri added. The cabra was a cupboard that dried clothes if coming in from rough weather, which was rare on their world.

"Okay, thanks." Yanda gave him a small smile.

"Did your disappearance have to do with your...abilities?" Omshi asked with a look of disapproval, as if her ability were stripping or exotic dancing.

"Yes."

"I knew you shouldn't have made a spectacle of yourself, rising past men in the ranks of surgeons." Omshi tussled with a slab of meat as if it were her mortal enemy.

"That wasn't it. I was detected from another galaxy." She wouldn't say "called". That might sound to her mother as if she went of her own volition. If she told them her mind had been taken over by the most powerful object in the universe, then directed onto the Lark where she was shackled in psi-blockers, her mother would still believe she went deliberately, and could have at least called.

"Did they grab you in full daylight?" Nedri asked quietly. He glanced at Zami, who was playing with his food, making neat patterns. "The hospital said you walked out without saying a word and never came back."

"I was given false information. And then imprisoned."

"They said your name wasn't on any ship leaving," her father went on, corroborating her thought.

"I'm sure my abductors kept that from the records easily enough." Yanda said, smiling at Zami, trying to reassure him as the atmosphere got tense. She fed him a bite of *sadi snips*.

"They." Omshi slammed her knife on the table. "Who are these people? What did they want with you? What did they do with you? Or have you do? If I can even believe this story of kidnapping."

"There's a very bad man, Kridenit." Yanda wouldn't say "mage". Magic was not in Omshi's chosen vocabulary.

"What did this Kridenit want with you?" Omshi demanded.

Yanda avoided saying anything that involved powers. Even bringing up her abilities had been risky. Omshi bought into her religious group's ideas on extra-sensory capabilities—that they were evil—and she seemed to get more fanatical every year.

"It's a long story, and I'm tired," Yanda settled on saying.

"So, who is the child's father?" Omshi asked.

Yanda started stacking their plates to clear the table, and stood. "He's Terlondian. I'm going to run Zami a bath, if that's okay."

"Are you married? Why isn't he here with you?"

Yanda carried dishes into the kitchen, Omshi hot on her heels.

"Bad enough we don't know Seiti's father. Now another?" she hissed. "What would the church say. You're not a...a..."

"What, Mom? A hussy? A harlot? A *bogoy*?"

"Stop with that language, Yanda." Omshi looked like she'd slap her. Instead, she picked up a plate with dark, moist spice cake slices. "Come have dessert." She returned to the dining room and served out bright orange cockleberry sauce and a dollop of whipped *lali* cream on each plate.

\* \* \*

Running water in the bath, setting toys bobbing, with a naked Zami leaning at her side, watching, Yanda breathed a sigh of relief. She stripped and sat in the bath with her baby. They played for a half-hour, giggling and splashing, Zami making fae globe-lights float over the surface. Yanda had never learned the skill from the Elves. Maybe she wasn't capable.

Whenever they quieted, Yanda heard murmuring from the den down the hall.

\* \* \*

When their skin puckered, prune-like, Yanda dried Zami and dressed him in his Elven snuggie. She put on her soft Rotoulian nightgown made from tree fibers. They were two of the few items she'd brought in her single bag from Terlond. She'd spotted a knit baby hat in the garage that would hide his ears when he slept. She slipped it on him, tying it under his chin. His ears were so delicate, they made no impression on the cloth that covered them.

Carrying Zami down the hall to what was now Seiti's bedroom—Yanda's, once upon a time—she called out, "Good night," to her parents.

"Aren't you going to come and give a kiss—chat some more?" Omshi called.

Yanda heard her get up and approach the door. But Zami was tired. His ability to settle the Elven whirling of his eyes, and glamour his leaf-shaped ears was waning. "Let's talk in the morning. We're pretty *scanda*." She hoped Omshi wouldn't be too offended. But she hated the idea of more grilling, more disapproval. Frankly, she couldn't bear it tonight. She closed the bedroom door softly behind them.

Shelves in the room were jam-packed with children's books. Yanda perused them as Zami worked his way along the lowest, fingers gripping the books and shelf for balance. He'd never seen so much reading material. They chose an old favorite, about a sprite who wanted to be human for a day. Seiti'd loved this book, the story, the illustrations on the plaz pages.

Her daughter was gone. Yanda had waited a year and a half to see her, to hold her. The last thing she expected was to find that her daughter had left home. Had their adoptive parents been watching her well enough? She had too much guilt in her own abandonment to take them to task.

Not wanting to upset Zami, she hadn't yet had a good cry. She settled Zami in the child-sized bed, in the pajamas he'd acquired in the elven forest, his only pair, and climbed in after him, snuggling up against the pillow to read.

Soon his lids drooped. She nursed him until his eyes slid shut and his lips grew slack. Then she slid his head onto the pillow and climbed out of bed.

Footsteps approached.

"Are you asleep yet?" Omshi asked. "Want hot *chaka*?" That's what they called a sweet milky drink from a cocoa-like seed of the planet.

"No thanks, Mama," Yanda said in a low almost-whisper. "Zami's sleeping and I'm about to follow."

"Okay. Good night." Omshi's footsteps moved away down the hall.

Yanda listened for her steps to fade, then pulled boxes and baskets from the high closet shelves. She examined every item. Then she started on the desk drawers.

Omshi cracked the door open. "We looked through all that," she hissed.

"I know, Mama. I just have to see for myself."

"Thought you were tired."

"I'll go to sleep soon." Yanda kept her eyes on the sheet she held—a homework assignment, hoping to discourage further conversation. For good measure, she flicked a meaningful glance toward Zami's sleeping form.

Omshi followed her gaze, a frown creasing her brow. At last, she pulled the door shut a little harder than necessary.

Mama, you've shown your growing xenophobia. Guess what? I'm Xentu. That's why I see through things. They told me more on Terlond about myself than you ever did. How much did you know?

Yanda pulled everything from drawers—mostly school assignments and drawings in notebooks. Seiti could write when she was three. She would be keeping journals. Yanda was sure of that. Did she bring them all with her?

Yanda dropped to her knees by the bed and reached between the mattresses. Her fingers found a thin sheaf of plaz—the base of materials used throughout the universe, sourced from plants and recyclables, made as thin as onion skin for paper, or hard and durable for furnishings and machines.

Tugging out the pile, Yanda studied the pages. There were lines of tiny neat writing, probably from a *buzz-pen*, which produced only read by a *decryptor*. Where would Seiti have gotten such a device?

Her daughter was clever. Few knew how to use encryption pens. Every one of them was encoded differently; the decryptors were programmed uniquely. Seiti would have taken the device with her. Even if she hadn't, Yanda didn't know how to program them; She knew of them from confidential patient records and recognized the encoding.

Maybe this wasn't the most recent plaz-sheaf, just one Seiti discarded. Since Yanda couldn't read it, she found a plaz holder, placed the sheets in and tucked it into her single bag, woven by the Elves. Maybe someone else could decode it and find answers for her.

Opening the door a crack, she listened. The house was silent. Tiptoeing to the bathroom, she gathered a few toiletries for her and Zami. She got the mail from the front hall, then slid back into the small bed next to Zami and tried to sleep. Hours ticked by.

# CHAPTER

# 2

**W**ith relief, Yanda watched dawn light touch the *dundri*—thin plaz blinds remotely controlled, suspended in air against transparent plaz windows. Quickly, she dressed and lifted Zami into his Elven carrier. She'd keep him in his snuggie, hoodie pulled up. He leaned his head to her chest, sucked his thumb and slept on. Easing out into the hall, she tiptoed down the main hall to the front door. Leave a note? What would she say? Obviously, she'd gone to find Seiti.

She eased the door behind them, hurried across the front yard to the sidewalk, and turned toward the town of Balyou.

\* \* \*

She stopped for *cuffa*—the coffee of her early life—and her favorite pastry, the *chepootle*—a sticky bun with sweet spices and fruit layered in—at Lo'l's Place, a café bakery that seemed to always be open. The smells and warm air as she pushed open the door reminded her of hanging out with friends during her school days.

"Yanda. Ha'n't seen you in long time." Old Lo'l smiled at her as he got her cuffa in a fat mug. His teeth were lined in gold, a rare sight indicating early life on another planet.

"That's true. How've you been?" Yanda asked him.

"Good. Good. Ye had another baby, I see."

She nodded. "Yeah. This is Zami." The place was empty, the only sounds the machines and small noises Lo'l made as he set down her steaming cup and pushed through swinging doors to the kitchen for a fresh bun.

He returned and handed her the pastry on a small plate. It wafted yeasty fragrance up to her.

"Thanks." She paid with *grest*—cash on Alland, used mainly outside of the city—then brought the hot bun to her nose to breathe it in. "Mmmm..." She chose a booth by a window and settled Zami on her lap, keeping his soft yellow hood on his head. The street was dark but for solar-powered lamps suspended at intervals that glowed in a light mist hovering above the buildings.

Zami's eyes drifted open and landed on the sweet treat. He decided he liked berry *chepootle* very much and wanted more, but Yanda suggested a healthier meal in a while would be a better idea.

Where would she fix meals? She had access to her accounts with a *sidu*—the handheld device she'd brought from her parents' home, but was it wise to use it and give away her location? Why was she hiding.

She had better ones at her apartment that could be encrypted to disguise her use.

# MARIE JUDSON

* * *

When Zami finished his small cup of *chaka*, she snugged him back into his carrier. Saying good bye to Lo'l at the door, she headed down the street. Wan light etched the buildings now. A few people moved about the sidewalks. Yanda had chosen a beret-type hat in Seiti's room that she pulled at a tilt to cover her face. She'd rather her parents did not know she was still in town. She didn't plan to return to the house until she'd found her daughter.

Beyond the town was nothing. All was flat. This being a terra-formed planet, it had never produced trees or oceans. Everywhere was flat, with an occasional low hill, tall grasses and bushes. A massive network of water channels webbed the planet, crossed by low bridges.

Church of the Vital Promise was on the next block, across one of said bridges.

Ironically, those with unique abilities—the very abilities the church spoke against—were said to gather in an annex behind the bigoted church. This underground group met at odd hours, so she'd heard. Some might be there now, before dawn. But if not, Yanda would wait.

She found the low annex behind, as expected, along with an extensive parking lot surrounded by grass fields.

Yanda peeked in the annex windows. All was dark inside. But through the back wall, she made out someone moving around in the church itself.

Planning to wait as long as it took, Yanda scanned the deserted-seeming area for a good place to settle in with Zami. At the edge of the lot stood a small shed of fiber-planks. Even at a distance, Yanda could see what was stored inside: tables, chairs, shade umbrellas for outdoor events. She strolled to the shed, thirty meters away and explored around it, as Zami babbled and played with a flexible plaz *woo-loo*, the planet's smallest marsupial.

"Interesting," Yanda mumbled to herself.

Zami's eyes turned up to her in question.

"There seems to be a tunnel underneath." She was looking through the wall and beneath the floorboards when, just before he came around the corner of the shed, she saw a man approaching.

"Can I help you?" he asked.

Yanda knew the man was special. He must be one of the underground. But where had he come from? She'd seen no one anywhere around. "I have abilities," she said.

He gave her a steady gaze, then with a slow smile, asked, "Do you now?" He was not committing.

"I heard that people with talents gather..." She glanced toward the annex.

"I don't know what you're—"

She pushed mind-speak into him. "I'm looking for my daughter. She's special, too. She may have come here searching for me." She shared, mind-to-mind, a thought-picture of Seiti—a recent one she'd seen in her parents' home.

He leaned against the shed, fixed her with unfathomable dark eyes, and said, "I'm Arc." Then, in mind-speak that was elegant, tripping along sweet and soft like music heard far off, he added, "You'd best meet with Cellin. I think she might have talked to a girl. Or she'll know if someone did."

Yanda glanced again at the annex, but he shook his head.

"A tunnel under this shed?" she asked.

He scowled, then appeared amused. "That's your talent?"

"Yeah, I see through."

He stared at her a moment. "You're dangerous. I've heard of you. Heard you would come. Yandawi?"

"How do you know that name?"

Arc glanced at Zami. "We need to get underground." He pressed his hand to a weathered board at the side of the shed. Colors appeared on the next panel. He tapped a code.

Zami twisted in his carrier, reaching as if he'd like to play with the buttons.

A smile tugged at Arc's mouth. A panel slid aside and he gestured for them to enter. He glanced before stepping in after them and tapping more buttons on the inside.

"So, the annex is a ruse?" she asked.

"We'll talk more soon." Arc moved a cabinet to the side. With a word and a touch, he revealed a door. They entered a small closet. Its floor descended. Zami took it all in calmly, supplying a float globe to light the enclosed space.

"Special little guy you have there," Arc said.

Yanda wondered if she'd been right to trust the man so quickly. What guarantee did she have? She pressed her lips to Zami's head and let a question melt into his mind, very private between them. "Should we trust him? Is he good through-and-through?"

Zami pushed on tiptoes, put his little hands on each side of her face and, his check against hers, thought, "Good heart man. Many olds."

She laughed, circling him with her arms to snuggle him closer.

Arc watched, pensive.

The descent stopped. Yanda had been imagining what

they'd see when they reached the underground level. She hadn't expected lively activity. As the lift door slid open, she caught a whiff of *cuffa*—not just any *cuffa* but spiced, like in Skarth's international quarter near the spaceport. As the opening broadened, a sight formed: humanoid beings in various stages of dress or undress, lounging on couches, sipping, chatting, laughing. The room quieted. There were glances and pauses in conversation that quickly picked back up. Some nodded in their direction with smiles and mental feelers, questing gently into the outer parts of her mind.

A tall, broad woman, wearing a bright wrap and headdress beckoned from a kitchen area at the back of the room. Arc led them to her. Intense energy sparkling in wise eyes, she reached out for Zami. Yanda had no trouble relinquishing him to the kind-vibed woman. Thick necklaces lay on her ample bosom and bracelets clacked on her wrists. Her walnut complexion creased with a smile. She brought Zami close, her large hands encompassing his chest. The two said nothing for a long moment. He dangled in mid-air, feet still, hands resting on her large arms.

Yanda came around to make sure he looked happy. He chattered away in mind-speak with this stranger, his irises whirling.

"Come. We can talk better down here." Cillen put Zami on a hip where he could play with her large colorful beads, and led them down a hall lit by lines of dim light, to a separate, quieter room. This one faced out into a crater where a vegetable garden flourished.

Being a planet with no trees, it was hard to hide anything. Yanda had never even known this crater existed. And no wonder. From the lot, she'd seen only grass stretching out to infinity. The crater had something like a shade cover over it. She thought it might be like the *dundri* blinds on windows that were held in place by magnetism. Narrow strips allowed full sun on crop lines.

Cillen bounced Zami on her lap. "Yes, Seiti was here." She reached into a pocket and drew out a buzz-pen. "She left this."

"Left?" So Seiti had been there, but was no longer. Yanda's heart sank into her throat and bile rose to her throat. She dropped into a cushioned plaz chair. Hope had risen, only for brief flash. Now it plummeted.

Cillen shook her head in commiseration. "I told her to wait. But she met rebels who promised they could find anyone in the universe."

Yanda gripped the chair arms, stomach churning. "Met them here?"

"Of course, most of our population here is made up of fugitives, from persecution, and worse. Not all call themselves rebels. I wonder if any actually do call themselves that," she mused. "I guess tech-rebel is a thing people claim. And those aligned with the movement in the outback."

Zami scrambled off Cillen and toddled to Yanda's knee. He stood in front of her, eyes searching her face. She pulled him up, giving him a reassuring smile and settling him in her lap as she'd longed to do. "And you let an eight-year-old just go off with them?" She tried to keep her voice calm. Think, she told herself. Don't lose your temper. You need allies. "Do you have contact with these rebels?"

"Tenuous. They move constantly." Cillen studied Yanda's face. "I don't mean to worry you. Your daughter is a marvelous being. So brilliant. So sad."

Yanda choked a sob.

Cillen leaned toward her and laid a hand on her arm. "She is strong. And we are strong. All you've come through? You will find her."

Yanda stared at this woman, almost hating her. Cillen had seen her daughter more recently, had learned enough of her to know her strength. Her eight-year-old strength. Much more than she, her mother, knew at this point. And what did she know about where Yanda had been, what she'd been through?

Arc watched the interchange, sitting across from them. "Would you like *cuffa*?"

Should she have more caffeine? "Yes, please." She had to have some of the spiced drink she'd been smelling.

"Shall I make hot milk for the little man?" he asked. "Perhaps a bit of brekkie?"

"That'd be great," Yanda said. "Why don't I come and help?" She stood with Zami. Though she knew she should dig all she could, she felt worn out by what she'd already learned, and by Cillen's powerful presence. She was also afraid of alienating the woman with her anger.

"No, no, you stay put." Arc gestured for for her to sit and turned away down the hall.

"There's a nursery. Perhaps Zami would like to play a while," Cillen offered.

This was quite an operation, Yanda thought. "I have to tell you. We came straight off the ship and glamoured a bit to get out of the station without being detected. So, we didn't go through the *froshers*. I don't frankly know if we carry anything other kids shouldn't be exposed to. We should maybe be quarantined."

"What a brilliant and generous confession. We have healing staff. Let me call someone." Cillen tapped at her wrist. A clear plaz band lit up. "Is Soni in?" she asked.

Yanda heard no answer but within minutes, a small-ish woman, tawny complected, with faint freckles and thick hair in several braids, stepped into the room. Her coverall hung loose on a wiry frame. Maybe she was young, or just small.

"*Sawa ninga*," she said to Cillen with a smile, her eyes serious.

Yanda liked this new person's look. All seemed like-able here, trustworthy. Was it a skill they had? To send out a pleasant, honest vibe? She hated to be so suspicious, but after all, the world had thrown her many curves in the past two years: she'd been kidnapped, raped, and kept from her daughter, whom she'd now lost.

Soni knelt in front of her, resting her hands first on Yanda's arms, then on Zami's. "Mmm," was all she said for a while. At last, she sat back on her heels. "We'll have to keep this little guy in nature a lot of the day. His system is craving sunlight, chlorophyll, and living matter in general. But otherwise, no disease. You, my friend—" she turned her eyes toward Yanda— "need cleansing. There's toxicity in your lungs and blood."

"I should have seen that. I'm…a surgeon by training and have been trained in sight for body work but didn't think to check myself. I don't know why I didn't see it in Zami."

"We are the last ones we see ourselves," Soni said. "I sense the healer in you. As a surgeon, I'm not sure you would have been trained in this type of diagnosis, though." She smiled.

"Have you ever worked with Elves?" Yanda asked, grinning back.

"No, but I've been many places. I can hear what the

body needs. I didn't mean to pry but when I was checking, some thoughts came through. I saw a beautiful Mingalean in your mind. Her system was very troubled by Terlondian air."

"You saw all that? *Ambas,* I learned to hide thoughts but I'm not doing a very good job." Yanda felt embarrassed.

Cillen clucked, as if to say, "Don't be silly. You can trust us."

Soni put a hand on Yanda's knee. "You've had many shocks. You're with friends. We only want good for you."

"Then I have to tell you, my adoptive mother is a member of that church." Yanda shot a glance upward. "She has absolutely no mind talents and never liked that I was unusual. I did not tell her I was coming here. She could be trouble."

"Omshi." Arc pushed through the doorway carrying a tray.

"Yes, that's right." Yanda felt relieved they knew, so she could say less.

He set the tray on a low table close to her. Soni scooted back and leaned against the wall.

"There's so much I want to ask." Yanda thought about her first conversation with Arc, how he'd called her Yandawi, said he'd expected her. "Maybe after Zami eats a little, I could take him to the nursery."

Soni said, "He should get some time in the garden."

"Perfect." Yanda knelt by the table and put bits of scrambled ploto egg with broken-off toast on a small plate for Zami.

"I wouldn't mind helping out there myself," Yanda added, then took a grateful bite of the eggs. They shared plant-based sausage, rich, with *sweet satiyati* and anise.

"We have to program you into the security," Arc mentioned, "so you can go out into Satarn."

"Is that the name of the crater?" Yanda asked, mouth half full.

"It is," Arc responded.

He seemed to give the two short words special meaning, making Yanda wonder.

Soon they were walking as a group down the hall. It curved, small windows sliding open as they passed, then darkening as they left each section.

# CHAPTER

# 3

At the next bend, the corridor widened into a bright, colorful room, with vibrant décor. Several young children played with toys on a large round rug at the center. Windows gave onto the lush vegetable garden. In her arms, Zami drank in the greenery.

"Can we go out there now?" Yanda asked Cillen.

Zami strained to get down and join the other kids. She let him slide to the floor. He'd been taking a few tentative steps on his own. She stayed close.

"Arc needs to calibrate the security on Satarn's entry points to your vibrations, and Zami's," Cillen said. "Let's talk a bit more in here."

They took chairs near the children.

Yanda dug in her bag for the encrypted plaz sheets and handed them to Cillen. "You have Seiti's buzz-pen. Can you decipher this?"

"I can't. But Jelat can. He'll be back tonight."

Cillen frowned in thought.

Yanda watched the children get to know each other. Zami was on his knees, helping to build a tower with a brown-skinned, round-faced girl, slightly older than him.

"What's her name?" Yanda asked.

"That's Colo."

Yanda held the decryptor Cillen had handed her, studying it. "I don't know where Seiti would have gotten it." Yanda took it, holding Cillen's intense gaze. "She's barely eight." Tears crept into the corners of her eyes.

Cillen nodded. Her expression was neutral but Yanda could not help feeling like a terrible mother.

Arc entered and nodded. "All set."

Yanda crawled to Zami. "Want to go out in the garden?" she asked.

"Want to," he said, clutching Yanda's leggings to stand. "You come too?" he asked his new little friend.

A woman, tall and lanky, had been reading at a table to the side. She glanced over as the tiny girl asked, "Go garden?"

"You may. I'll come too." The woman left her book and joined them. "I'm Merem." She held out a light brown hand.

Yanda took it.

"And you're Yanda." Merem smiled, showing lovely teeth, two of them set with tiny green and blue gem stones.

Yanda felt a spark in her mind. No one had ever before entered her psychic space with that particularly lively effervescence. Zami felt it, too. Yanda could tell as he turned to the woman. Merem winked at him.

What was that energy? Yanda pondered as they filed out into the filtered sunlight. Alland's pale yellow sunlight was what she'd always known, until Terlond's orange sun. In comparison, Alland's was bland, but comforting.

She associated the rusty orange of Dondar, Terlond's main city, with toxic air.

She walked between corn rows holding Zami's hand. He stared up at them, never having seen cultivated food growing in rows. He'd been into the Elven forest to gather mushrooms and taken along to harvest fruits at the edge of the woods. The imprisoned fems had tried to scavenge seeds to plant in their desolate walled yard, but he was only an infant then.

Yanda dropped to her knees by a plot of onions, radishes, and other root plants. Zami dug his hands into the soft, rich earth, grinning.

Arc brought a bin of tools, gloves, and kneeling pads. "We're preparing a new bed over here."

She got up to follow. "What will you plant in it?"

"We have options. *Muldoo sprouts, catatuga roots, dali frond, sadi snips.*"

"Is this the season for all that?" She tried to think if she even knew the dates.

He grinned at her. "It is. But you probably know we have a long growing season on Alland. Lots of leeway."

"Ah, well, I was a city dweller, in Skarth." Yanda smiled, self-deprecating. "I grew some herbs on my windowsills."

Arc chuckled. "Which herbs?"

"I tried to grow *satiyati*." Her face crinkled. "Did better with *kodok*."

"That's impressive. Not easy to grow that one." Arc picked yellowing leaves low on a plant.

Cillen came out. "Jelat is arriving back late tonight. Can you meet with him then?"

Yanda glanced from Cillen to Arc. "I think so. But..." She strained to smile as she said in a small whisper, "I'm not sure where I'll be tonight."

"I assumed you'd stay with us," Cillen said. "You're welcome."

"There are rooms?" Yanda asked.

"Yes, you haven't seen the whole place. There are more hallways." Cillen plucked a snap pea and crunched on it.

"How did all this come about?" Yanda waved her hands, indicated all around them.

Zami sat contentedly scraping up soil, making hills and holes next to her.

"That's many stories." Cillen laughed merrily as she started back toward the hidden doors in the side of the crater. "Let me know when you want to see where you'll stay," she called over her shoulder.

"Actually, maybe now. This guy will need a nap soon." She scooped him up. She looked at Arc with his tub of tools. "Sorry. Can we take a raincheck?"

"Absolutely."

She hurried after Cillen. "I want to earn my keep. Please let me know what I can do."

Once they'd gone back inside, door whispering a snick-snick—open and shut—Cillen studied her minutely. "Do you have anything in mind?"

Yanda huffed a laugh. She could draw stones from across the universe; join with an Elven circle to hold up a protective dome over their forest; pull an object out of a body with her mind; see through walls or microscopic tissues; travel in spirit; read minds; block hostile thoughts. Was any of that useful to them on a day-to-day basis? "I'm not sure what you might need, but I could harvest food for dinner, help prepare meals, watch kids here in the nursery."

"I'm more interested in the litany of skills you just ran through your mind," Cillen said with a wry smile. "We don't require stones drawn from across the universe, but there is healing to do. We also have a power circle, to hold some of the security of this place, combined with tech. It might be something you could learn to participate in."

"Oh, yes." Yanda wanted to learn how technologies extended magic and vice versa.

"Um, Zami, when I work..."

"That will never be a problem. There's always an adult in the playroom."

Yanda bridled, keeping it hidden. She did not know these people, yet had to trust them. They were her only known link to Seiti. Yet, let herself meld into a power circle, leaving Zami to others' care? There was so much interest in him. Cillen had communed with him out of Yanda's mind reach. That seemed rude. Like with Zamani, a tie formed that did not include her and she railed against this loss of control. While loving to share her special son, she feared where that could lead. "Of course, I'll help any way I can. I'd love to learn more. I imagine the Circle might hold security over your crater."

Zami had again joined the other children on the rug.

"May I ask why you located this refuge so close to a church bigoted against our kind?"

Cillen sat and watched the children stack. This time he played with a boy toddler slightly younger than him.

"Better to stay close sometimes. The Church is complex. And our kind are very much involved with its workings. It would not do to leave such a planetary-wide power unchecked. We also benefit from them at times."

"Oh." Yanda had a growing feeling that this Cillen

was no small fry in the doings of Alland. Why was she in this backwater of a town?

"Much easier to see from a distance sometimes," Cillen answered without Yanda needing to speak.

Yanda had grown used to sorting thoughts in hidden recesses of her mind before she let them fully bloom in consciousness. That way, they could be tucked behind the wall before ever being detectable. Any thought Cillen read was intended to be shared. Or that was her hope. "I have much to learn about this world I grew up in." She shook her head ruefully.

"You're not old, Yandawi. You focused on your surgeon skills. And you had no one to guide you in these more esoteric abilities."

"Did you people know of me, from infancy?" Yanda's eyes stung with the asking. "Arc said something."

As if she manifested him, Arc drifted toward them.

"A bedroom has been set up for you," he said.

Staying overnight in this underground shelter seemed to snap suddenly into reality. Yanda found the thought stifling. Could she come and go at will? "Can I go into town if I want?" she asked.

Arc and Cillen exchanged a glance, and Yanda's heart sank.

"We try to only go out—" Cillen started.

Arc jumped in. "—there's a screen for you to check. Whenever it shows green, you can go into the crater area. The town. You have to try to come out at different points so the shed and crater don't raise suspicion."

"I understand." Yanda wanted to be a good guest. It was a refuge, after all.

The only sounds in the room were of kids playing and

Merem speaking softly to them.

Then Arc said, "You and Zami, in particular, want to try not to be seen or detected anywhere on this planet, Yanda."

Yanda's heart hammered at his sudden honesty.

He went on, "We've scrubbed any visuals from the optic surveillance between here and Skarth, and in the spaceport. Jelat can tell you more."

Yanda gripped the chair arms so hard they made grooves in her hands and ached, but she didn't dare let go. Her breaths came shallow as though breathing any harder might stir up more trouble.

"You can't think your abduction was not news here?"

Her eyes widened.

"It was kept out of the press but in some circles, there's been a great deal of speculation." Cillen was looking at him with warning in her eyes but he went on.

"Also, about your Elven friend in the ship docked there in the city."

"You've…" Yanda was shaking. She glanced at Zami, who played contentedly, fitting together parts of an elaborate apparatus.

Following the direction of her gaze, Arc said, "More important than the visuals, we've scoured sensory readings. There would be great interest in Zami's skills. I hope we got them in time. We did detect you from fairly early, getting off the Lark. But others could have, too."

Yanda's thoughts cast out over the possibilities. "Maybe you'd be able to find where Seiti's been. If there's so much surveillance catching me and Zami and Tenali."

"There are so many ways to hide if you know how."

"How would she know how to hide? Could Jelat check

for her? For her mental register?"

"You can ask him tonight." Arc touched her elbow. "They've set up a healing bath. Soni's in there now calibrating it."

Soaking in a healing bath sounded like what she needed after all this. Tight knots ached in her shoulders. She stood. "I want to nurse Zami a little, let him sleep. He could have a healing bath after me? I imagine mine might be set differently or I'd go in with him."

"You're right," Cillen said. "Soni will have a bath appropriate for Zami after yours. You could join him in it. It'll just balance him from the long space journey."

I should have thought of more greenery on the ship, Yanda berated herself. "I have to learn to detect his body's needs better. I guess because he showed no signs of distress…"

"You and Soni will work together. You can learn from each other." Cillen opened a door to a hallway opposite where they'd first entered.

Yanda asked Arc, "How is air coming in? It feels fresh."

"We have a wonderful aeration system, a network of ducts. I can show you a blueprint sometime."

"Fabulous," she said, though of all the ways to spend time there, she wasn't sure that would top the list. She knelt by Zami and reached out her arms.

He looked up, reluctant.

"We'll be back," she said, "Or…could he bring this to our room?" she asked Cillen and Merem, indicating his half-formed construction.

"Feel free. Gather more pieces into a basket." Merem pointed to a stack by the wall.

They filed into a narrow hallway. Yanda carried Zami,

clutching his creation, and Arc followed with gathered plunka-toys.

"How many rooms are here altogether?" Yanda asked.

"Uh...thirty-seven?" he called to Cillen, ahead of them.

"That sounds right," the big woman answered.

"They loop all around the crater?" Yanda asked.

"Around *Satarn*, yes," Arc said.

Yanda detected a note of reverence in his voice. She stopped and turned to him. "Is the crater sacred?"

"Oh yes." He smiled and faint visions wisped through her mind, of ceremonies long ago, with sweet-smelling flowering vines, bonfires, dance, and song. She sensed a compelling scent, like the *sidu* roots Elves gathered from mountainsides to burn as incense.

"Satarn," she said, giving the name a respectful intonation. "Are there still ceremonies?"

"At times," he said, wistful. "Not enough."

She hoped she'd see one.

"Soni tells me the bath is nearly ready," Cillen called at the next bend in the hallway.

"I'm going to breastfeed this guy," Yanda said, bouncing him as she walked toward Cillen.

"Your room is just ahead." Arc moved past her and opened a door.

When Yanda arrived, she peered in. Filtered beams of sunlight rayed through opaque panels, green where it shone through hanging plants.

"How is this room getting sunlight?" She had expected only artificial light.

"Outside your room is a small courtyard with skylights," Arc explained.

"With the same kind of covering as Satarn has?"

"Yes. We blend into the landscape," Arc said, head bent toward her.

"How could all this be done with no one noticing? It seems unfathomable."

Cillen had come back to stand with them, looking in. "Carefully. At night. Over a long, long time. And very skillfully."

Yanda felt a blend of awe and skepticism as she stepped into the room. After all, she'd grown up less than a mile from here. She let Zami down, along with his basket. Zami was drawn to light striking strings of crystal beads, making rainbows across the floor, and crawled to them."Don't pull too hard," she said as he reached for them.

The room was cozy, with weavings on the walls, a fluffy quilt on the bed, homey touches on dresser and table. Throw rugs softened the floor. "Is it possible to go into the courtyard?" she asked, fingering the bead curtain led to it.

"Any time you like." Arc stepped across the room and pressed a pad. Clear plaz doors slid open. A small fountain played, and plants grew around the edges of the square patio.

"We'll let you relax. I'll come in a little while to take you for your soak, and someone will watch Zami, if that's okay with you," Cillen said.

Yanda felt dread. Zami had been raised by ten Fems his first months. They were all captives together, in one room. There was no reason for ulterior motives. Here, she felt layers of intrigue and hidden purpose. She had to warm to the place, though, even if by sheer force. These people were her only hope at the moment. "Alright.

Thank you. Maybe they can bring him where I can see him from the bath though?" She sounded pathetic but so be it.

Cillen rested a hand on her arm, her large brown eyes full of compassion, but a thousand forms of calculation as well. Or so Yanda suspected. "It'll be better if you fully participate in the healing." She turned; she and Arc left.

The door slid shut and she and Zami were alone.

# CHAPTER

# 4

**W**hat was this healing anyway? Just hours before, she'd come from her parents' home, only knowing she had to find the place she'd heard about, where those like her gathered in an annex off the church. She'd found the underground shelter—and discovered Seiti *had indeed* made contact here. What had led her there? She'd found no clue at the house. It might be in those encrypted sheets.

She settled pillows at the head of the bed and put Zami to her breast. He barely needed it anymore, would soon wean himself from her, but in these trying times, there seemed to be little enough she could offer him.

His eyes drooped. It must be early afternoon by now. As they cuddled, Zami drifting off to sleep, Yanda ruminated more. Had her daughter sought out this place or had they approached her? Yanda hadn't thought of that before. Perhaps she'd find out more from Jelat tonight. Was he the one who put Seiti in touch with the rebels? For the first time since she'd been back on her home planet, Yanda had the freedom to think further about next steps. Maybe Jelat would help direct her toward finding Seiti, but she should get to her apartment in Skarth.

"I could try to find what I need, with my ENAC 370, not depend on others." She'd purchased a sophisticated computer not long before she was abducted. Few in the medical fields depended solely on their employers to provide the latest innovations throughout the universe. The ENAC series had nearly unlimited reach and capacity. If she could get to it.

A twinge deep inside made her wonder if she'd done the right thing coming to these people. Was she inside a great web as bad as the government, merely coming from a different angle? When Omshi said Seiti went to a medium or spiritualist, Yanda had assumed the only way to find people outside the mainstream was the annex. Should she have taken more time, laid low, tried to pick up the trail of her daughter while remaining independent?

A tap came on the door.

Yanda gently scooted the sleeping Zami over, created a pillow barricade around him, then went to answer.

Soni stood in the hall with a younger woman. "This is Beril," Soni said, voice low. "Is it okay if she stays with Zami while you're in the healing baths?"

"How long will it take?" Yanda asked, combing over Beril while she gave her a friendly smile.

"You should stay until the monitors say you're done. Beril will have a *fiti*. You can call her." She handed Yanda a small disc.

Seeing it had a clasp, Yanda hooked it on her shirt. She watched the door close, obscuring her son from view.

"Come. You'll love the bath." Soni smiled at her and softly tucked her hand into Yanda's arm, tugging lightly. "This'll be you-time."

Yanda resisted that idea mentally, thinking *Zami-time is me-time*, though she came along.

The room they entered, after a zig-zag of corridors, was darkened, with indigo light seeping around an opaque screen.

Yanda pulled off her boots and slipped on booties, as directed. They crossed the room, her feet sinking into deep carpet. Behind the screen, a large oval tub filled with blue water hummed. A scent of herbs, pleasant and earthy, permeated the air.

"Strip. The temperature should be just right but let me know if it's too hot or not hot enough." Soni smiled, gesturing toward a table for clothes and belongings. Yanda snapped off the *fiti* communication and removed the rest. She climbed the tiled steps and descended the other side, finding a safe shelf above the end of the tub for the communication device.

As she submerged, the steamy water bubbled with effervescence. She sank to her neck. Her body rested, angling down until her legs were raised by cupped devices that molded to her shape. She let herself relax, breathing slow and deep.

At first, she noticed Soni cast in blue from the lights on a panel of switches and buttons. Then she let her mind drift. It spiraled into a cosmos that at first seemed empty. Slowly, on a level so unconscious it could barely be perceived, she became aware of a thrumming vibration in her bones. She perceived it as part of the healing in her cells, her bloodstream. A distant thought told her it was cleansing her, breaking down lung contamination, swishing it away. "What about my head?" she wanted to ask. Surely there's toxicity there, too. I should have underwater breathing equipment and submerge completely.

Incrementally, the drumming in her marrow formed into a voice. She'd communed with this voice before. Ash-don. Elf Stone of the Neyla. "What are you tickling me for, good sir?" she found herself saying with a burbly chuckle. Her mind and body were in a pure state, open, receptive. But not stupid.

"I think you'll want to come to me. This is not for my need. It is for yours."

"*Ambas*." Was this happening? She was not at a fully conscious level, and the spirit of Ash-don slipped away, as her body, in the healing fluids, demanded she rest more completely in its hold. She released the last remaining bit of conscious thought.

\* \* \*

In her room, wrapped in thick soft robes, Yanda sat on the bed watching Zami crawl around the apparatus he was building, sit and add to it, crawl again. Giddy, she took slow even breaths into her newly cleared lungs. She hadn't been aware of the congestion—it was not enough to make her cough, but enough to keep her breath too shallow.

Later, she would send her sight down into her lungs to see, but for now, she had to enjoy her euphoria. "I think we'll need to go join the others for dinner at some point," she said to her boy.

He turned to her, delicate leaf-shaped ears pressed close to his head where his curls obscured parts of them. His Elven eyes swirled at the centers, barely perceptible from a few feet away. "What we eat?" he asked.

"I haven't any idea," she said, squashing an urge to giggle. She tucked her feet under the robes and curled on her side to face him, wondering what color his skin might take on later, or if it would stay the creamy golden brown it was now. She hadn't asked him to hide his elven features from the Satarnians—that's what she'd decided to call them, in her mind, until they told her another name. For her, the whole endeavor down here was based on trust. They had to trust her and she them.

"Mommy happy." Zami crawled to the bed and pulled to standing by her.

She kissed his silken cheek. "The bath made me feel good. I want you to have one, too."

"Take toys?" he asked.

"I'm sure you can," she replied automatically. "I'm tempted to languish here but we should go out there and join the others."

A small device on the wall showed the time as mid-afternoon. She flicked a button and put in Cillen's number.

The older woman's voice came through the small speaker. "How are you feeling?"

"Good. Am I needed anywhere?"

"No, you rest, take your time. If you need reading materials or anything else, please let us know. And if you'd prefer to eat in your room…I won't expect anything from you today. We can start a schedule tomorrow."

"I don't mean to be at all discourteous or ungrateful, but you do know I'll leave soon to find my daughter." Yanda did not want any misunderstandings. And after eighteen months of captivity like a jail sentence, she would not be held in anyone's clutches.

"I do understand that, *meezy*. We will learn things

when you're able to meet with Jelat tonight. In the meantime, you had said you'd be willing to do healing work, and maybe mind-meld on the security duty. I will only impugn you as you are here, by your own will, and when you need to go, you will be free to go."

Yanda knew exactly the distance they were apart. The length of several rooms, back in the greeting area with kitchen, where they'd originally met. Yet she felt the other woman's thought, *I know you were incarcerated until recently, through no fault of your own. I know how you've waited to be with Seiti, and been prevented from it.*

"Very well. Yes, put me on a schedule as it suits you, for tomorrow, and we'll see, day to day," Yanda said. "And I'll come out to dinner. It's good for Zami to have more than just me around him."

"It's good for you, too, *lassa*."

Yanda could tell this last term meant "young mother" to Cillen. "Yes," she answered, flipping off the unit, brain too full of thoughts to compose a longer response. "Come, let's explore the courtyard." She reached her hand down to Zami and they walked outdoors into the small square patio.

One could almost believe they were in nature, with all four sides covered in vines. Light shifted in the breezes that were passing above. "I want to see what this looks like from up there," Yanda said. She could not tell exactly what she was seeing above her, from her seat on a wood bench. "We'll have to investigate." She set Zami down.

He immediately began to explore the patches of soil that grew flowering foliage.

She dipped her fingers in the water that rippled and splashed from the small fountain.

Immediately the memory returned, of Ash-Don calling to her. Though she knew it was not the same as when Shalt had drawn her across the universe, desperate to be restored to wholeness, her belly clenched at the feel of the immense stone rumbling in her bones.

What was the Great Stone trying to tell her? "I think you'll want to come to me," it had said. Something about it being for her need. What need? Could it possibly be able to help her track Seiti? When the two Elven circles combined in the final battle on Terlond, Ash-Don had had access to her mind. Had the massive sentient rock detected her daughter? It was a dizzying thought.

Yanda realized her baby boy stood at her knee, excitedly pointing and chattering to her about his creation, a tall plunka-toy construction he must have wrangled out into the courtyard. It was elaborate, stunningly so.

Yanda knelt by it, arm around her son. "Haven't you made a magnificent thing, Za-Za," she praised. He turned to her for a kiss and her heart swelled with the joy of being his parent mixed with heartbreak of possible dangers they faced.

Yanda heard the tiny com inside their room: Cillen's voice called them to dinner.

Yanda stood, hand held out to Zami. "Shall we go eat? Maybe we should bring your magnificent palace inside." Together they lifted the plunka-toy framework. Maneuvering it between them, they moved toward the door, Yanda backing. "It's been a day. I should have called Tenali. Do you think, Button? I'm not sure what's secure though." She was mumbling, half to herself, now, feet stumbling over the door sill. "I suppose I can ask Jelat tonight."

Structure safely on the rug again, she said, "Let's eat and then see about a bath for you.

Do I have anything for you to put on for evening meal?" She dug into her bag, woven from natural fibers from the Routoulian, Elven forest, with appliqued designs on the sides in rich earth colors: gold, rust, indigo, burgundy, teal. "Ah ha!" She drew out a corduroy overall, tree-bark textured, and long-sleeved hoody. "The very things." When he was dressed, she put forest green boots on him and checked him over, tugging at the fit. The adjustable straps were at their limit. "We'll need to stock up on new clothes in Skarth. You're growing out of what we have."

\* \* \*

The evening meal passed amicably with a group of eight or so, expanding and diminishing as residents came and went. The white mash tasted like a cross between potato and cauliflower. Yanda chose plant-based strips of brown faux-something, with gravy, and veggies from the garden, especially piling on her favorite sauteed *catatuga roots* and *sadi snips*.

Conversations were about the daily running of the place. Yanda listened, learning something of the roles, such as errand runs to neighboring towns. This entailed tunnels and starting onto the road when well out of Balyou, taking varying routes at randomized times. All of it took planning on data screens; some of this was accomplished during the meal.

Dessert—small mounds of custard topped with bright crimson sauce and flaked coconut—dwindled and clean-up began.

Yanda asked, "Can Zami have that healing bath? And I wonder if we could borrow some pajamas. Maybe do a wash?"

Merem answered from the sink as Yanda carried a stack of dishes toward her. "Let's go to the playroom. Soni's gone, but she'll return soon, and Colo still has energy to get out before she'll sleep. We can scare up sleepwear for you two."

Grateful, Yanda nodded, watching Zami lead Colo toward a stack of books on a low table. Kitchen nearly clean, the four headed to the nursery. They found a few adults and kids in there already.

"We have card games the kids love." Merem showed Yanda choices on the shelves. "Do you know how to play Salters?" She picked up a deck and set it on a nearby table.

"'Course." Yanda snorted, recalling her days as a local girl, playing for chuta-sticks behind the school.

Having settled Zami with the other children on the central rug, Yanda joined Merem at the small square table and fisted roasted duddle-nuts from a bowl set in the center. She settled, feeling a smidgen of homecoming for the first time since she'd arrived back on Alland. "I've heard the name Pedore. What is that? Or who?"

Merem looked up from shuffling, as if surprised. "That's this place. It's us. We're Pedoreans." She grinned. "There are some other names. I'm sure you'll hear them."

"Like what?" Yanda asked, glanced at the kids playing chase around the rug.

"Moles," Merem said, suppressing a smile as she brought over a colorful card deck and some 9-sided dice.

The three parents in the room chuckled as they took leave of their kids. One said, "Beril's going to be here in a half hour. You okay 'til then?" to Merem.

"Yeah, yeah." Merem waved them out the door to go to their shifts.

# CHAPTER

# 5

**S**o, where'd you grow up?" she asked Merem when they'd played a while, with occasional breaks to attend to the kids.

"A smaller town than this," Meren answered, mysterious.

"Called…?"

"I don't think you'll have heard of it."

"Try me."

"Dalaton." Meren gave Yanda a sideways look.

"Nope. Never heard of it." Yanda slapped Merem's hand before retrieving a pair of cards she'd won.

"Cillen and Soni are from even tinier villages close to Dalaton. They barely have names to anyone outside the settlements, so all the area's peoples are referred to as Dalatoneans."

A squabble among the kids broke up the game. As Yanda and Merem sorted out what happened, Soni strolled in wearing a synth-sara-skin jacket and carrying a helmet, the edges of her hair mussed as if blown back hard.

She tugged off gloves, saying, "I heard we might be ready for another bath, one for Zami?" She looked flushed, eyes bright, from a motorbike ride, Yanda thought, taking in the helmet and gloves.

Yanda straightened up, Zami standing with one arm around her knee. He was not one of the kids in tears, seemed to have just been observing. "That'd be great," Yanda said to Soni. To Merem she asked, "About borrowing clothes?" She lifted Zami into her arms.

"I'll take them to the clothes closet," Soni offered to Merem. She led Yanda, with Zami, down the hall they'd taken before. A side corridor took them to a walk-in closet lined with neatly labeled shelves filled with clothing of all sizes.

Yanda's eyes widened. She picked through Zami's size for nighties and some day-clothes, then found a few things for herself.

"All set?" Soni asked.

Yanda turned to her, load tucked under one arm, the other holding Zami.

"Here." Soni tugged a cloth bag from a high shelf and held it open.

"Are these clean or should I ...?"

"All laundered before they're put in here," Soni assured her.

As Yanda followed back out into the hall, she sniffed surreptitiously at the clothes. They smelled fresh, of lemon soap and maybe outdoor drying.

The three went down a further hallway to a different bathing room. This one had multiple tiled baths, steam rooms, and saunas at the back. Soni set her helmet on a bench.

"We don't need to do this right away," she said, watching Soni unzip the heavy, lined jacket.

"I'm good. I'll pop on scrubs and wash my hands and face. Might be a few bugs on it from riding the ride." Soni washed up and pulled on yellow scrubs, then came to set dials by a pool. "The water will be ready in a moment if you two want to get undressed. Unless you're too sick of bathing."

"Never." Yanda stripped herself and Zami.

Soni dipped in a hand. "Temperature should be good."

Yanda stepped down in with Zami. Soni brought bath toys and they lingered in the shallow pool until Cillen's voice announced on a speaker, "Jelat's here." She asked Soni to show Yanda to the Cone. "Beril's coming for Zami."

"Righty-ighty," Soni responded.

Yanda tugged on sweats she'd found in the community closet, and put Zami into pin-striped pajamas with a cartoon *woo-loo* appliqued on the front.

As Beril entered, dressed in a snug long sweater over soft pants that reminded Yanda of clothes she used to have. She'd yet to return to her apartment where she'd left a full wardrobe.

Yanda sighed for things left behind, then kissed Zami's cheek as Beril crossed the room holding out her arms. "Snacky and a game of shatari?" she asked, invitingly.

Zami let her pick him up, but gazed back at Yanda as they left.

\* \* \*

The Cone, on the far side of Pedore, was a round room surrounded by lit-up panels.

Jelat turned from a monitor and nodded to her without smiling. He looked more like a boy than a man, with light blond hair, peachy cheeks, and thick glasses that magnified his eyes.

"You can get Yanda back to her room?" Soni asked. She looked weary. This had to have been a long day for her. Yanda wondered where she'd gone.

"Yeah. 'Course." Jelat waved Soni out.

He didn't show a lot of social graces. Maybe he's on the spectrum, Yanda thought.

"Nah, just worried. And sleep-deprived."

Yanda sat by him. "I meant to hide that thought." Studied his face. Was he hurt?

Actually, she *had* hidden it. So, he'd done some digging. She'd do the same. She entered his mind, just a bit farther than was distinctly polite, feeling daring. Immediately, she had a sense of order to the extreme.

Before she could find anything of interest, Jelat's mouth quirked. "I'll tell you anything you want to know," then, in mind-speak, added, "especially once we get to Skarth."

Once we get to Skarth. What did that mean? They were going to her city? And why would he only tell her then? His expression was inscrutable. His meaning was clear. Even here, he wouldn't risk what could be detected—overheard—from mind or voice. What side did that put him on? What sides were there?

"I should be worried about what I say or think here?" she asked, in protected mind-speak, directed tightly from her mind to his.

He swiveled toward a keypad and tapped in the

information. "In some sense, this is a 'cone' of silence." He hooked his fingers like quotation marks. "Hence the name."

"In some sense. Okay. Am I communicating safely with just you right now?" She wondered if he could tell. She'd grown used to her teacher, her guide, Shouma, on Terlond. Shouma who could detect what was heard, how far, by whom.

"You are." His eyes barely twitched in her direction. "You've had some training."

"Some, yes. Haphazardly conducted as needed." She drew in a long breath. She hadn't realized how much she needed to speak about her time in captivity, to help put it in perspective.

His head barely sketched a nod. "I want to hear it all." He tapped a few additional keys, watched data appear on a screen, then snapped it shut and turned to her. "We have a short time. I've set the air around us into a shimmer. You have coded plaz?" He held out a hand.

She felt thrown off guard. Who should she trust? She knew nothing about this strange young guy with his baby face and knowing eyes. With a mental shrug, she reached into her bag, pulling out the covered plaz and buzz pen.

His eyes widened. Hadn't Cillen told him? Yanda didn't believe he hadn't already tried to use it. What was that expression?

He took them in his hands delicately. "Do you see this at the top? Around the edges?"

She peered where he indicated and saw nothing.

"Here." He reached for a shelf and handed her a pair of lenses. "Try now."

Once she had the glasses on, a pattern appeared.

"This type of plaz is not made on this planet, and is

rarely imported. Same with the buzz." He flipped a miniscule power-on tab with a thumbnail and, setting the plaz on the long desk module, ran the buzz over it. Shaking his head, he said, "I'll need an attachment, in Skarth." He turned up his palm. "We have about a minute and a half left."

"How would my daughter get this?" Yanda said with growing unease.

"I think it may have found her."

That's what Yanda had feared. "Do you know who...?"

He shook his head. "She's eight, you say?"

Yanda nodded, foreboding aching in her stomach.

"Eight in Alland years," he muttered. Alland was large and years were slightly longer than the universal norm, but not by much.

"What are you thinking?" Yanda asked.

"Do you mind me asking who her father is?" Rose patches colored his cheeks.

Yanda stared at him, taken aback. It was a likely question, yet no one had asked it in a very long time. Her shoulders came up in a defensive shrug. "Someone I met. Late night. Drank a few too many." She felt him probing her mind, as if the answer wasn't good enough, but this time she was ready with all of Shouma's teaching. He didn't get any further.

His lips barely smiled as he slid the plaz back into its cover. "I don't suppose you'd let me keep this." He glanced up. "For safety."

She shook her head. That was her only tie to Seiti right now.

"Let me at least put it into something more substantial," he requested.

"Sure. Thanks."

He slipped the plaz into a hard, shiny holder, placed the buzz pen in a compartment built into it. Then he ran his finger around an overlapping seal and handed the case to her. "Nothing can penetrate that. We'll leave for Skarth tomorrow."

"We? Who?" she asked, standing.

"I'm sorry. I should have put that differently. Can you leave for Skarth in the morning?"

Her lips pressed down, wary. "Me and my son, you mean?"

"Yes, of course, you and Zami. With me."

Hearing his name, she bridled. Was her Elf child famous throughout the place? How far?

"Cillen has told me a little about you and your son. And you may know Arc and others know more, even before you came back." At her expression, he added, "Not many. And Arc's a friend. An ally. Don't worry." He stood as well, his head even with hers.

*Not many.* This was not a comfort.

Jelat said good night at her door. "You need to leave the courtyard shut at night. Security has been set." He glanced at her bag where the dark case nestled.

"You think people would want to get this?" she asked.

"Oh, yes."

Was her daughter hiding important information? Or was it urgent to someone to find her daughter? Dread filled her, knotting her intestines.

He touched her arm. Intense energy thrummed through her, even though it seemed like a kind gesture. "We'll talk more in Skarth," he said, low-voiced.

She nodded, drawing in a long, slow breath as he turned and strode quickly down the hall.

She heard laughter behind the door and tapped lightly.

Beril opened, still chuckling. Zami stood in the middle of the room, poised to run. They'd clearly been playing a fun game and both seemed out of breath.

Yanda's heart clenched, even as she felt relief that he'd been happy and occupied with her away. Of course, she wanted him to gain independence. Of course, she loved to see his world broaden. He spent his first year doted on by a circle of fems from throughout the universe who had powers, then was embraced by Elven society for a time. Coming back to her home planet, she'd worried about a possible nomadic existence, hiding out, the two of them. But so far that had not been the case.

She entered the room and sat on the edge of the bed. Zami came to her and peeked in at the new black, shiny case, eyebrows high, as though he felt drawn to an energy in it.

Beril said good night, quietly closing the door after her.

"What were you playing?" Yanda asked.

The boy scrambled up with her help and did his best to convey the game's rules into her mind. It sounded a bit ad-libbed. "Well, it looked like you had fun."

"Had fun wiff Beril," he agreed.

"We're going on a trip tomorrow," she said, rummaging through the clothing bag for the nightgown she'd earlier acquired.

"We go trip?" Zami asked.

Yanda was glad he didn't always resort to mind-speak since she loved hearing his sweet, piping voice.

"Yes, you'll see the city where Mommy used to work. We saw a little of it when we landed at the space port and came here, but now we'll go in and see my apartment. My old home."

"We safe?"

Had he picked up that they might not be? Was she projecting that idea? It scared her sometimes, that he may be intuiting way more than she could monitor, but she would just have to trust, as he grew, and make sure they communicated. She should have done that in his earliest months and she would have known he was in touch with his bio-father, the Elf leader, Zamani. But for the infant mind, it was just part of his world. He didn't think to mention it, and she missed the clues.

"I've wondered that too, Button." She snapped the area at the tummy and back where the pajamas connected.

Being a precocious child, Zami had started letting her know when he needed to be held to tinkle or go number-two at a very early age, so diapers were not an issue. When he could sit and there was a potty chair available, he used it.

In bed, she snuggled Zami close and lay pondering the next day as he drifted off to sleep.

# CHAPTER

# 6

At dawn, Jelat buzzed the wall panel. "Meet at the dining hall?"

She strode toward the young man—young looking, she couldn't be sure of his age—having passed through the nursery area where early activity had begun. Zami rode on her back in his Elven strapped affair, and she carried all they had with them under one arm.

"You look loaded down. Can I help with something?" Jelat reached his hands out to her.

She knew he was being helpful—at least that was the thought he projected—but she had the uptight notion that he just wanted the plaz sheet. "Have you already eaten?" she asked, sliding the carry-all to the floor but not releasing hold of the strap.

He said, voice lowered, "The way we're going, there's a fabulous morning pockets place not too far along. I thought we could stop there." She figured he didn't want to insult the chefs so spoke quietly.

"Okay. Do they have veg stuff?"

"Oh yeah!" He nodded vigorously. "I'm vegan. You won't believe the fare."

"I heard that." A large freckle-faced man set his plate down behind them. "This scramble looks tasty, though." He sat and shoveled in a bite.

"Smells great, Storven." Jelat called out toward the kitchen, then reached for Yanda's bag. "May I?"

She heaved a quiet sigh. *We're all going together,* she thought. *I have to trust him.* He shouldered her belongings next to his own flat carrier and led the way to a door near the lift.

Jelat's handprint opened a panel, which shushed behind them. They stood in a tunnel.

"Anyone else coming?" Yanda asked.

"For now, it's the three of us," Jelat said, as they proceeded downward. Lights came on by motion detector along the way, leaving blackness behind.

Zami played with her hair, head nestled at the back of her neck.

The side panels shifted to rougher hewn rock and earth as they continued on. "Wow, the network of tunnels just keeps going, doesn't it?"

"They may have explained that we enter the main roads at different points, and at varying times?" he asked her.

"They did. So that's part of the purpose of these routes. To make it harder for anyone to notice that Pedore exists?"

"You got it."

In a quarter of an hour, they arrived at a row of motorbikes. "Have you ridden a *sedpod*?" he asked her, pulling helmets out of a recessed closet.

"Oh, yeah. I kept one in Skarth for trips out of the city." Yanda felt a burbling elation that she'd get her own.

He maneuvered a colorful one—peacock green and canary yellow—backward, holding it for her. When she came to take it, he found helmets for her and Zami. "Here." He helped her arrange Zami in front of her with a special harness.

His *sedpod* was dark red, forest green, and black. He slipped a leg over. Once he'd settled his helmet, he keyed on the vehicle. It was silent, then gave a low hum as he accelerated forward.

Yanda flipped a switch, bringing her bike to life, and pulled out behind Jelat. Zami sent elated messages into her mind as they picked up speed. In a minute, the tunnel filled with light and they rode out into a cornfield. Navigating a wide center lane, they came to a dirt road and took it, merging onto a small highway. Zami sent her mind-messages about all he was seeing: a bug that hit his visor, the feel of the wind against him, every sight and smell.

"Sun funny color," he said as the pale disc slid from behind a cloud.

"Yes, different from the orange one of Terlond." She pulled up closer to Jelat. "Will we be able to shield our identities when we reach Skarth?" she asked him in mind-speak.

"Yes. I'm going to do that. I'll project different identities for you and Zami."

"I'd like to get into my apartment," she said. "Can I do that without raising suspicion? I mean, we don't want anyone to know I've returned, right?"

"That's where we're going," Jelat said.

Yanda paused a moment. "To my apartment?"

"Yes."

She searched her mind for any other information she might have missed, then probed his, what she could reach of it. All she saw was her front door showing the correct address.

"Here's the place. Pockets," he said with enthusiasm, and veered off into a roadside parking lot.

The roadside café was active. "Are we safe? Are you already disguising us?"

"Yes, your mental registers. I'll bring you a menu. You'd best stay out here, all the same."

Would she and Zami be hiding themselves everywhere? Well, if that's what it took to find Seiti. She looked around. They'd parked at the end of a row of vehicles: *sedpods, gallihoes, denivans*. All the usual sizes for varying numbers of passengers. Bamboo and bushes ran along one side.

Jelat returned with a plaz menu and she picked out mushroom and *sossi*-curd pockets for her and Zami.

"Want sadi-snip fries? They're to die for." He grinned. He seemed so much more amiable on the road. Maybe he'd gotten a good night's sleep.

"That'd be great, yeah."

When he'd left, she checked around for cameras. Not seeing any, she almost pulled off her helmet, then thought, "Don't be lazy, Yanda," and set her detection skills into motion. She sent her senses out around them. "I bet this place can't afford too much surveillance," she said to Zami. "But the gov can. They have bots flying. One will pass here in 30 nanoseconds."

Sure enough, a drone hovered overhead and she was glad she hadn't removed their helmets.

"Head hot," Zami complained.

"We'll get back into cool air and probably stop in a safer place to eat," she coaxed, just as Jelat exited the building.

"Looks crowded in there," Yanda said, before thinking.

But, of course, he knew she could see through walls. He quirked a smile. "Yeah. Let's get down the road a bit with this." He tucked a plaz bag with the Pockets logo into a compartment behind his seat.

They rolled at a low purr out of the yard.

"A drone went over," she thought to him as they motored in tandem down the country road.

"They'll be searching for your register, your mental identity, which I've obscured, overlaid with someone very different."

Vatu could do that, Yanda thought, yearning to see her friend from her time of captivity on Terlond, her Mingalian companion with cerulean head nubs and amphibious eyes, and the softest warmest temperament she'd ever encountered. She wondered if Vatu had returned to Mingal, her small planet covered in oceans, at the farthest edge of the known universe.

She almost asked what that identity he'd given her. But it wasn't the most pressing of her thoughts.

Soon they turned off into a green tunnel of vines. She barely kept on Jelat's tail when he slipped off the highway without warning. They traveled a short distance, deep in foliage, to a layby covered over by a lattice and fruit-bearing vines.

Jelat parked and Yanda eased up beside him to make use of the sheltered tables.

"Is this place a secret?" she asked, unfastening Zami and lifting him to the ground. He peered around, curious.

"To most, I'd say. It's not on maps." Jelat set the steaming pockets on a table and stepped over a bench to sit.

Yanda sat opposite him. Zami forgot about wanting to explore when Yanda unfolded the food Jelat passed to them. It had a tangy intriguing aroma, tantalizing, with exotic spices. Yanda tasted it, then put a little in front of Zami on the waxy wrapper. "Yum."

Jelat dug in and only nodded in agreement as he chewed a large bite.

"Do you think we've drawn anyone's attention?" she asked.

"We haven't." He spoke with certainty, shoving a mushroom into his mouth and continuing his concentrated consumption of his pocket bread.

"Can I let Zami stretch his legs a little before we go on?" Yanda asked, as they finished eating and crumpled their packaging back in the bag.

"Sure. We're better off entering the cit with increasing traffic so we may as well delay."

Letting Zami scramble to the ground, Yanda pulled a squishy ball from her bag and sent it sailing toward him. He sent it back toward her with his mind, giggling. She ran around the side, letting it chase her before she snagged it from the air.

Jelat added to the game with circles of light that he sent around the ball. The rules got more complex as all three of them caught the disks, sending them around each other. They collapsed on a bench laughing and panting.

Back on the bikes, the road widened into a larger thoroughfare, and Yanda saw tall buildings in the distance. "Our disguised identities will get us into the city undetected?" she asked Jelat.

"We'll still take an underground route. I don't want these bikes on any system."

Underground route ended up being a series of subterranean ways that Yanda had never known existed under her city, beginning with an exit into the far outskirts, navigating a rough and tangled web of slums, busy with activity and a variety of denizens, until they drove into what seemed like a garage. A group of men stood to one side, clothing dark and shabby, headwraps, studs and piercings—a generally tough appearance Yanda might have found menacing, except they ignored them.

They drove into a freight elevator and dropped several floors, where they rolled out into a tunnel of gleaming tile lit by eerie light.

"This seems like an arduous way in. Do you do this every time?" Yanda asked.

"I'm taking extra precaution." Jelat seemed wary, which didn't comfort Yanda.

The tunnels took many turns, sometimes around pipes and power boxes, as though they penetrated the very workings of the city.

"What if you came down here and one of these was closed, blocked?" Yanda thought Zami had fallen asleep, head against her collar bone.

"We'd make a new way. There are alternative routes."

They'd spent maybe forty-five minutes in this maze when Jelat took a sharp turn and descended a sloping pavement. He stood before a wide sliding door. Yanda realized there must be facial recognition somewhere in it though she saw no key pad or sensor. The door scraped open and they rode their bikes into an area that could hold ten vehicles at the most. There were a few sedpods and bikes. Lights came on by motion detector.

Yanda knew where they were: deep below her building.

"We'll take a maintenance lift to your floor," Jelat said, drawing a satchel strap onto his shoulder.

Yanda shifted the sleeping Zami into his regular carrier, picked up her bag and followed Jelat into a large elevator.

As they approached her door, she said, "You're sure this...I mean, entering my flat is sure to set off a lot of alerts." Next to her apartment, she stared through the wall. "There are people in there!"

"Yeah. I didn't know how to tell you. Let's get inside and I'll explain."

Her heart thundered. Strangers, in her home? Why?

# CHAPTER

# 7

S he fumbled in her bag for her ID card that would key her in. Then remembered. "I don't have any of my IDs. It was…."

"That's okay." He pressed his hand to the middle of the door, where there should not have been any sort of access panel. Yet the door popped open.

Yanda checked around warily for cameras as she entered her own flat.

Three men and a woman sat at desk and table, appearing at ease in the space. They glanced up, nodding briefly as they worked away on computing devices.

Jelat closed the door. "As far as any cameras read, we're maintenance. Cleaning crew. Approved."

"I see." Yanda flicked a hand toward the others. "And they're in here because…" She kept her voice calm, neutral, but of course Zami could read deeper; he pushed himself up to examine her expression. She smiled, kissed his cheek, rubbed his back in the carrier.

"I'll explain." Jelat stepped toward the dining table.

The woman had risen and started toward Yanda, hand held out. "I'm Kishan. Welcome home, Yanda." Her voice was a warm contralto. Her dark hair was twisted onto her head with small carved pins.

Yanda slid her hand into the other woman's and immediately received a flood of friendly information, an outpouring of ready sharing. She now knew some of the woman's history.

"This must be Zami." Kishan turned and gripped the boy's tiny hand. "My son is about his age."

Computing devices were set aside.

"We have some *cuffa* brewed." A man of middle years, neat clipped beard, looked sheepish as he hesitated halfway to the kitchen nook, most likely awkward that it was, in fact, her kitchen.

"I picked up pastries. They're on the sink." A second man, this one with hair so orangish red it almost hurt the eyes, waved casually toward the other room that opened onto the dining and living areas. He seemed tall even seated, legs stretched far under the table.

Yanda set Zami down and walked with him to the kitchen. This was not how she'd imagined showing her little boy the home she'd made for herself once she left university. She'd imagined touring him around, pointing out her plants and photos. Thinking of that, she glanced through the pass-through opening to the other room and realized her ivies, *aglaonemas* and hanging *bromeliads* were perfectly healthy. She'd expected to find an apartment full of dead things.

More for her comfort than Zami's, she hoisted him up and spoke quietly to him. "Are you hungry?" She opened the cold storage, curious if anyone had stocked it.

Sure enough, there were leftover containers, fruits and juices. She checked the frozen section, out of curiosity. It was well lined with healthy frozen meals. But nothing she would have ever stocked. She closed it and picked up a berry *floofle bennie*. "Let's split this. We had a pretty good breakfast."

Zami watched avidly as dark syrup leaked onto the plate where she'd sliced. She washed their hands, and carried it in. Settling Zami by the couch, kneeling at the low table, she returned to put hot water on to heat.

Since she'd chosen a more child-friendly part of the room for her toddler, Kishan moved to the couch. The others followed, gathering around the *cuffa* table.

Yanda returned with herbal tea—one of her favorites that she'd not tasted in nearly two years, made of sweet and savory spices, along with some exotic, healthful roots and leaves. She sat at the end near Zami who calmly looked around at the four strangers as he licked syrup and drew with it on the plate. Yanda leaned over to bite into the oozing *floofle bennie*, from a bakery she and her fellow workers at the hospital frequented.

"So," Jelat said, squirming in his seat. "You probably want a good explanation for why we're in your apartment."

"You knew I was going to be gone a while. It was a place you could set up, disguising yourselves as maintenance and cleaning, already funded by my ongoing account. Less financial trail to cover." She shrugged. "Makes sense."

Kishan put her hand on Yanda's arm. "You don't mind?"

"No. You kept my plants happy." Yanda grinned, a half-smile.

The tall, flame-haired man gazed at her steadily. His

sturdy frame ate up the chair and a good bit of space beyond it.

The third man was ferret-like, with a small pinched face and high forehead. He fidgeted constantly.

"How long have you been occupying this space?" she asked.

They glanced at each other.

Then Jelat answered, "Days after you were abducted. We didn't want the space to be invaded by the those who could gain too much data on you."

Yanda listened to all this, mouth open in shock.

Jelat straightened in his seat. "Ark has told you we've known of you a long time, hasn't he? Well, always. Some of us have known since you arrived on Alland."

"Us, who is us?" Yanda asked as alarms clanged in her head. What did he know about her arrival? She wished they'd had this conversation, just the two of them. It was a rather large audience for information that felt this personal. She glanced at Kishan and found that the other woman's eyes were on Jelat, a slight frown creasing her brow. Warning? Disapproval? Sensitivity to Yanda's feelings?

Yanda wanted to know what he knew, but she wouldn't ask him now. "Yes. He hinted that."

Zami held up his arms for her to help him onto the couch. When he'd settled beside her, she dug in her bag for his favorite toys.

Flame-hair leaned forward, elbows on his knees. "I'm Ilan."

"Nice to meet you," she mumbled, not sure yet if she was at all glad to make any of their acquaintances.

"Yanda, we had to get through all the data you had to make sure you weren't compromised. Not just on your devices that were here in the apartment, but in the walls."

"In the walls?" Her voice was a studied neutral, not belying the adrenaline pumping through her.

"We found a lot," said the ferrety man.

"And removed it. Well, changed the feed." That was the middle-aged bearded man. Ollie, had they called him?

Jelat took back over. "We put in a standing order for cleaning and maintenance as if you ordered it before you...left."

"That way we could safely make this one of our stations." Kishan spoke softly, again touching Yanda's arm. Her eyes pleaded with Yanda to be comforted, that they had no nefarious purpose there.

"Well, again, I'm glad you've kept my plants watered and...I don't mind that you made use of the space. You may as well." She took a sip of tea, cleared her throat and added, "Will you be here, day and night?" Her voice squeaked a little with tension.

The others exchanged glances.

"Uh." Jelat shifted again. "We don't think you should be here alone. Besides...you don't plan to stay long, do you?"

She *had* imagined at least a day or two to herself before getting on the road again. "Do you have a lead on the rebel camp where my daughter is?"

Ollie fidgeted with a small device, glancing at her, at the others, away.

"Um. We do," Ilan blurted when it became clear the other man wasn't about to say it.

There was hesitation in his voice, Yanda was sure. She made an instant decision. Why stick around? She didn't have a home here. "I want to go. Today if possible."

"Today won't work." Jelat's brusqueness surprised her, even for him. "Preparation can be made for tomorrow. If you don't mind, Kish will share your room. We have cots for the four men out here."

Apologies for invading her space were over. This was now command center and she'd better get with the program. That was the tone she heard. Jelat leaked very little of his more inner thoughts. By careful design? Yanda had to wonder about the baby-faced man. Was he kind? She drew in cross-legged on the couch, bringing her back up straight. "What does tomorrow look like then?" If brusque was the game, that's where she'd meet him.

"It looks like full ID creations for the three of us for exiting the city. We have to set up the rendezvous which is a delicate operation, to avoid endangering the rebels."

"Refugees," Ilan inserted, shoving a hand through red hair that flopped into his eyes.

Yanda studied him. He wore thick-lensed glasses.

Jelat nodded. "I stand corrected. Most are more on the run than actively trying to disrupt the system."

This Yanda wanted to know more about. She'd always wondered. Didn't there have to be more like her? Yet talents were hidden, suppressed, outlawed. Information was so far underground, it had been nearly impossible for her to find even the least hint that there was a place of refuge. The Church of Vital Promise. And she'd never gotten up the nerve to explore it until desperation over her missing daughter.

"You're not going without me." Ilan's shaggy red eyebrows furrowed low as he faced Jelat.

"Aren't you on Circuit?" Jelat asked, testy.

"Sheron is coming on at 06:40. Next four diurnals."

"Sher's interning." Jelat didn't look happy.

"Let's order take-out," Kishan suggested.

The debate was still going on at mid-dark when Yanda carried a sleeping Zami to the bedroom and laid him at the center of the bed while she took a shower. When she came out, Kishan had made a cot by the wall and already lay on it, fiddling with a small hand-held device. She'd set a few things on a small cube she used as a side table.

"Night," Yanda said, folding herself under the covers of her bed and snuggling Zami in with her.

"Sleep well." Kish put out the upper light with a flick of her hand.

Hmm. Something they've installed? Yanda wondered. She never had a unit like that. Or was it magic Kish had?

Now, in the dark, Yanda could ponder. What did she know? Her walls had been filled with surveillance by the Sinisay—the part of the government that monitored talent. They outlawed its use, while illicitly sequestering powers. Deset, counter-group of talents, could override Sinisay's presence, installing their own. What did that mean for her?

Tomorrow they would meet the rebel refugees. Ilan said they had new information on Seiti. That's all she could focus on as she listened to them argue about the following day. Round and round the thought ran: when will they tell her what they know? Because it was Ilan who told her they knew something, she found herself hoping he would come with them. Jelat was so cagey. She liked the big red man's outbursts, as if he couldn't contain a secret that might hurt her. Or maybe she just wanted to think of it that way.

As she was slipping toward sleep, Tenali came into

her thoughts. Tenali! Yanda's eyes flew open. Dared she try to reach him from here? After all, the underground rebels who'd taken over her apartment had made these walls safe, hadn't they? But she would need to know how to use that safety. Should she ask Jelat? A tiny, niggling doubt rose in her at the thought. He and Arc knew about her arrival on Alland. Logic dictated that they knew about Tenali, the Lark captain. How much did they know about him? About her, for that matter. And was it wise to tie them in with him? Why was she even wanting to reach out to him? Because she felt herself a prisoner in her own home, not knowing what she could and couldn't do. Not knowing who to trust. It was as almost as bad as being locked up in Krid's citadel. If she accepted it, that is. Wasn't her advanced laptop on the side table?

Hadn't Abdil, fellow surgeon, installed Da-Lam, an encrypted program so that she could research any other psi talents involved with surgery without raising red flags? What else could the program do?

She listened to Kishan's breathing. It seemed steady, like sleep. Delicately, she slipped into the woman's mind. Yes, she slept.

Just as softly, Yanda climbed from her bed, knelt, and brought the computer to the floor where light would be blocked. She tapped the silent keypad. Once in Da-Lam, she navigated as far as she could get toward locating Tenali or the Lark. When she hit a dead end, she closed her eyes for a moment. A grid formed in her mind. She opened her eyes and tapped keys. A series of layers opened, one, then another. She touched the interstices, knowing now what the interface could tell her. Was this related to other forms of sight she'd been developing?

A last rayed star blazed on the screen, and a map of

all ships docked at the space port on Alland filled the screen. The Lark was not among them. Well, she knew that. But what could she do with this information? Find histories? Merne could look at ship manifests.

# CHAPTER

# 8

Yanda ran her hand a millimeter from the display. Tiny notations appeared near each vessel as her hand came close.

She rolled onto her back on the carpet. Can I encrypt my mind through the program, to seek Tenali's mind? As she lay, eyes closed, she saw the program working, establishing a unique identifier for her. The answer was yes.

She was communicating with an AI system. She saw how she could send messages as codes, similar to translating thought into another's mind. Her breathing quickened as she established the environment for long-range search. She'd done that with the Great Stone, searching for Shalt's fragments across the universe. Now she sent out a call to Tenali.

Nothing.

Why would he leave the planet without contacting her? Maybe not wanting to risk endangering her and Zami. She had not tried to connect with him before this.

But what made him go? And where had he gone? She felt her throat knot up.

Gradually, she eased out of the AI environment, taking slow, even breaths to maintain control.

And lay thinking. This was an environment she was good at. It suited her skills. She knew somehow that she had only been in a small part of the entire web raying out into infinity. But she also had a sense of the full extent and, with this same sort of knowing, was sure she had crept among the signals, leaving no trace.

She hugged herself, excited. This could mean a lot for her search. She itched to go back in. But, too tired, she crawled into bed.

\* \* \*

Early the next morning, Yanda got up, leaving Zami sleeping, and checked the bathroom. It was available and she showered in her familiar cubicle, with the settings that read her mind.

Toweling off, she dressed for journeying, in the flight jacket she'd acquired at Pedore. She pulled on her Elven boots, which she noticed with chagrin would soon need resoling. "Bugger." She had brought the case with the plaz sheets and decoding stylus in with her. She paused, noting the distrust this indicated, but shrugged. "Better safe."

Yanda entered the main room to the smell of *cuffa* brewing, the kind with spices she loved, sold only from the market near the space port.

"You're up early," she said to the tall, broad, flame-haired Ilan.

"I was hoping you would be, too. Would you want

to talk? Up on the roof?" He handed her a travel mug and lid. "I don't know how you take it."

She noticed an accent, very subtle. Where was he from? "Sure." She dolloped *Arspat tinas kahay*, a plant-based milk from a hybrid Allandian grain.

She used to go onto the roof of her building and had considered growing a garden up there, as others did. But there'd been little time, with her surgery load and leaving on weekends to see her daughter. Her stomach clenched as she remembered, once again, that Seiti was missing. She took a hearty gulp of the strong, soothing *cuffa*, and looked out over the city.

"It's nice up here." Ilan blew and sipped from his mug, large shoe propped on a low wall in front of the bench they shared. "I had a view like this on Qontaq."

Yanda started, and stared at him. "You're from Qontaq?"

He nodded. "I am."

His burly frame matched Bonden's. Dele was more delicate, willowy. "I have two friends from there," she said, excitement rising at this connection with two of the highly skilled companions from her captivity.

Ilan looked surprised. "Here? On Alland?"

Yanda shook her head. "No. We were together on Terlond, held prisoner." She touched his tree-limb arm lightly. "Is it safe to talk up here?"

"Where I am, it is safe," he said soberly, then amended, "If I'm conscious." A small self-deprecating smile showed surprisingly small teeth with slight over-laps. "What are your friends' names?"

Yanda's brows rose. "You think you might know them?"

He shrugged. "It's a small population."

"Bonden and Dele. They have great skills." Her throat

tightened with the memories. "They saved us."

Ilan bowed his head, his large hands clenching the mug. "They've been missed."

Yanda thought he might crush the cup. Her brow creased. "You knew them?"

"Only by reputation." He eased his grip and took a swallow.

Jelat's voice came from the door-well. "I thought I'd find you up here."

Yanda's heart fell. They'd come for Ilan to tell her something out of range of the others. Surely what they'd shared wasn't what he'd wanted to convey.

She felt Ilan's unique mental register quickly establish a one-to-one link with her. "It's okay. I'll be traveling with you."

That's all. He must have detected her concern. Why would he assure her he'd be there with them? What was he trying to say? That she wasn't safe with Jelat?

They greeted Jelat as the pale sun made its first appearance on the farthest edge of the city. Jelat found a weathered chair. Just as he brought it over, settling with his *cuffa*, Kish poked her head out from the stairwell.

Ilan and Yanda laughed as all made their appearance on the roof, their amusement tinged with frustration.

Kishan shoved open the door and stepped out holding Zami in one arm, a cup of *cuffa* in her other hand.

Yanda jumped up to help but the woman shook her head. "I've got him." Her hand wrapped around, gripping the baby's thigh. As they crossed the rooftop, Zami looked out over the wall at the city vista, just as she'd seen from her apartment window years before—tunnels between tall buildings, shuttled shooting through, picking up early morning light.

Yanda's heart swelled to see him; her throat tight-ened. *I should be holding him for his first view of my city from above.* But she scolded the thought away. "Thank you for bringing him up."

Kishan sat on a low wall, well inside an outer one. "You could leave him with me, you know," she said, bouncing him and sipping her warm morning drink.

That was all Yanda could stand. She stood and came to get her son. "Thank you so much. He'll stay with me." She scooped Zami up and brought him back to the bench.

"To go to the rebels?" Kishan's voice was a tad rep-rimanding. "You go get your daughter, then come back here. He can stay here safe 'n sound."

Jelat lifted a tempering hand. "We'll protect him, Kishy."

Ollie shoved open the access door with a screech. He held a bakery bag. They all scrambled for their share of a variety of oozing *floofle bennies*. Yanda picked out lemon for her and Zami to share. She had barely started chewing when Jelat said, "Eat up. It's already late to get started."

\* \* \*

Bags hanging from their shoulders—Yanda's containing her ENAC 370 and the plaz case, another for their few clothes—the three adults descended in the lift to below ground, a level that showed on none of the building's wall directories. Yanda held Zami tight.

Despite Yanda's fierce surety when challenged, Kish had gotten to her. Was she being selfish dragging her tod-dler along? Did the other woman know about something Yanda should be aware of? Was it what Ilan had wanted to tell her?

The three straddled bikes, Ilan climbing onto a tall, broad model.

Before they drove out of the last garage level onto the crowded city street, the men cloaked them and their bikes. They rode in silent, float mode, a pressure system that required battery charge but was silent.

"This seems faster," Yanda thought to Jelat and Ilan. "Are we on schedule for a rendezvous?"

After a moment, Jelat responded, "Approximately. But with these people, things can change at any minute."

"Reassuring," Yanda thought. She checked the fastenings that held Zami in front of her, facing out, his little helmet allowing full vision, at least to the sides.

After a quarter hour weaving through downtrodden neighborhoods similar to those they'd traversed the day before, they entered a highway. They were invisible even to each other, though they could feel their companions' minds. Zami, being in contact with her, was visible to Yanda. They rode three across, in a V-shape, Yanda in the middle.

In just over an hour, numbers appeared on her wrist device. At the same moment, as they were passing through farm land, Jelat and Ilan pulled ahead and swooped left down a dirt road, then right along a rutted trail, maybe made for a tractor. Plants grew taller, and then a little-used path forced them to single file. The narrow trail twisted and turned.

They floated a few inches above the rough path, vines and branches catching at their legs. Then, dipping into a tunnel, they sailed downward.

Soon, a light flared ahead of them. A narrow-faced man stood alone, youngish, maybe her age, medium height and build, dark hair held back in a rust-orange kerchief, hoop earrings. He had the rebel look, she thought, canvas jeans and vest looking worn. It was hard to tell much about him, but she thought he seemed nice enough.

They came to a stop by him. Jelat thought, into her mind, "This is Setoin."

"I'll get these returned," Setoin said. "We don't want them tracked."

"We've been shielding them," Jelat assured him.

Yanda looked around.

"I came alone," Setoin said. "Others are deeper in the tunnel. How long did you pay for?" He gestured, indicating the bikes.

"We own them," Jelat said, sounding slightly impatient. "No one will identify them."

Setoin opened an undetectable wall panel onto a hollowed-out storage, and rolled Ilan's bike into the black maw.

"We could take these all the way," Jelat protested.

Yanda held out her bike and Setoin took it.

Jelat still gripped his. "Are you confiscating these for the cause?"

Setoin grinned and Yanda saw that one of his back teeth glowed. In the fleeting glimpse, she thought she saw marks. Symbols?

Zami sent a globe light above Setoin, as though to help his mother see the teeth better.

"That's nice. Who made it?" Setoin asked.

"Me," Yanda claimed, not wanting too much interest in her boy's Elven talents.

They heard voices approaching.

Yanda pressed her check to Zami's and said into his mind, "Hide your special ears and eyes, okay, my sweet?"

Her son twisted to face her. He'd transformed his ears to the small seashell shapes common to non-Elf children, and settled his eyes to calm aquamarine irises; he knew she loved that color. She kissed his nose, throat tightening.

"I not mind," he said cheerfully, still in mind-speak. "Maybe you learn to make Elf ears someday."

She grinned at him. "Possibly. I'd love to transform."

Jelat gave up his bike just before several others of varying heights and appearances stepped through a tunnel opening some yards away. They approached and fist-punched all around in greeting. One was older, grizzly; the other three—male? female? it was hard to say—seemed young. Yanda assumed they all had special abilities, for their minds were well shielded.

Ilan towered over the group, taking in exchanges with quick glances though he smiled amicably. Yanda had to wonder what he was thinking. Maybe he was busy keeping them all protected from psi-spies. He'd said their communication would always be safe in his presence. Well, Shouma had taught her to make a dome of concealment. What more could he do?

"Let's get a move-on," Jelat said.

Setoin asked, "It's just her and the kid going on with us, isn't it?"

Jelat stepped closer to Setoin. "We want to make sure they're safe, and that she gets the information she needs." He glanced at Ilan. As team? Or adversary?

After Ilan's strange behavior that morning, Yanda couldn't help but wonder.

Setoin studied them. "It's not that simple."

Jelat tilted his clever baby-face to one side. "Why is that?"

"Because we're not the ones with answers. None of us has seen her daughter."

"But you know someone who has."

"Yeah." Was that a coy glance Setoin sent off into the dark?

Yanda listened closely to all thoughts she could catch—fleeting snatches. Nothing clear. Setoin sounded like a native Allandian, though his energy carried something unfamiliar, something very off-world.

"I think we're all you've got. Am I right?" Setoin turned to Yanda. "You'll have to come to our camps. We'll liaise to discover what you need."

"Yeah. I'm going with them." Yanda almost glared at Jelat. If he lost her this chance to find Seiti... Turning back to Setoin, she asked, "You don't want Jelat and Ilan to come? I'm fine with that."

Ilan shuffled his boat-sized boots with undisguised agitation, staring meaningfully at her but saying nothing.

"They can stay with us one more day," Setoin said. "We'll shelter overnight at the farm."

The other rebels stood in wide-legged stances, waiting.

Yanda's palms sweated; she slid her hands under her arms. "That's fine with me." She stared away from Ilan's penetrating gaze that was trying to catch her attention.

# CHAPTER

# 9

"Alright. Come." Setoin led them into the tunnel from which the others had exited.

Soon, at a branching, he took a right, then a left. They arrived at a small underground stream. Lights shone on bedding, and a fire burned low.

The young rebels dropped cross-legged by the fire, joining a comrade who'd remained behind. Earth smells permeated the close air of the tunnel, also the green scent of algae in standing water close by, she thought.

"We can't stay here long," Setoin said. "Are you hungry?"

"We haven't been on the road that long," Yanda said, still standing.

The rebel group set about clearing their encampment and they moved off down the tunnel. Soon they came to another storage built into the wall. Inside, long covered objects were in a stack. Setoin and another rebel extracted five and unwrapped them. "Swizzers" they were called.

Yanda thought of sleds she'd seen photos of, gliding on snow, which only occurred on the poles of her planet.

"The last tunnels won't accommodate bikes," Setoin explained.

An eager young rebel climbed on one of the *swizzers* and flipped switches. It came to life with a humming sound as it rose off the ground. "These are the controls," he explained.

Yanda came close and studied the lit-up panel.

"Go. Stop. Raise. Lower. Speed up, down." He demonstrated each.

"You might want this one." Setoin showed Ilan to a longer version which would fit his frame.

Jelat jumped on one, and in seconds had shot down the length of the corridor and back, eyes bright. "Okay. Let me lead." He got on his and moved ahead.

"You couldn't do this very well pregnant," Yanda commented as she stretched onto a dark red *swizzer*, Zami tucked under her chest on his tummy. She carefully made them rise, then move forward.

"We go fast now?" Zami asked.

"Not too fast," she said, tickling his side.

He squealed, excited.

They moved out, leaving behind three of the rebels.

Lights on the fronts of the *swizzers* lit the way as they started single-file into a smaller tunnel opening, Setoin ahead, Ilan directly behind Yanda. This passage would not even allow comfortable walking.

She rested her chin on one fist, gripping the front with the other, grateful for padding. Zami's eyes grew wide with wonder and elation as they sped along.

Setoin sent a mental message back to Yanda, "We'll be going to a lower level before we exit onto the surface.

We recently had a breach in security so we're being extra cautious."

Yanda shivered, nuzzling Zami's back as they whizzed through, a foot or two off the ground.

"How dangerous is it, to have my little boy here?" she asked.

"Lots of exiles have children," Setoin answered. "Children suffer the consequences of our blind system as much as anyone."

Wouldn't that be the truth for Zami, looking the way he did, she thought.

The blackness smelled of ancient soil.

Setoin's mind again came into her thoughts. "What have you learned so far about your daughter?"

Yanda hesitated. She'd just met this guy. But she needed help. "Not much. She showed up in the underground shelter at Balyou and plaz with encrypted notes. She went in search of a seer and ended up with rebels, or that was rumored."

"You spoke to the person who sent her to us?"

Yanda was stumped a moment. "I don't think anyone thought she went to you. I think she was told of a sort of diviner among Wanderers who sometimes travel with your lot. I'm not that sure about it." Yanda felt dread as it became clear to her what a very sketchy enterprise this was. Had she pinned down Cillen and Arc enough on the details? Yanda rested her cheek on her fist and wiped a tear's trail keeping her eyes ahead.

"Do you want to stop and rest?" Setoin asked.

"I'm okay."

"How far is it?" Ilan asked, broadcasting the question to all of them.

"There's a house. Part of the underground. We can

ride up to it. We just need to approach from a back route."

"That'd be good." Ilan sent a clear message about what *swizzers* were like to ride as a large man.

Yanda huffed a laugh but cut it off with a squeak as they dove deeper down, made a quick right turn, then soared upward. Yanda felt the difference in the air before taking in open land and lights in the distance.

"Uhh…" Ilan groaned as his swizzer settled on the ground and he stiffly unfolded from it. "How much longer on these?"

"The safe house is just over there." Setoin pointed at soft lights Yanda had noticed, faint in barely discernible mist. "Again, there's no need for you and Jelat to continue on."

"No one knows of this place?" Yanda asked.

"We're far into wilderness," Setoin answered. "There's little effort at surveillance out here and, so far, this house has never drawn attention. We're trying to keep it that way." He lifted his *swizzer* and walked toward a low shed among other outbuildings just taking form in Yanda's vision. "We'll need to set shielding as we approach, and hold it all the time we're there. We can take turns sleeping. I'm pretty fresh. There are friends who will watch as well."

"Oo. Can we wash up there?" Yanda asked.

"Yeah." Setoin ducked his head with a shy grin.

Yanda took note with interest. This was a side of him Yanda hadn't seen. "I feel like I have bugs in my hair and on my neck." She climbed awkwardly off the now-inert swizzer lying on the ground. She felt an unaccountable laugh bubbling up as she swung Zami into her arms. Was it the air here? Making it out of the city alive? Or Setoin's pronouncement of no surveillance in this country area?

"We'll be fed and can bathe," Setoin assured them as

he stored the *swizzers*.

The other rebel, whose name Yanda hadn't caught, helped him carry hers over and put it away as Ilan and Jelat brought theirs.

"It's a small farm and occasional inn for anyone who stumbles out this far."

"Is it all alone?" Yanda asked, bouncing the now-sleepy Zami.

"No. There are a few other tiny establishments in the area. They help each other, but keep to themselves as well, and protect each other's secrets."

"So, all very innocent," Ilan asked. "Good set-up." He sounded skeptical. He usually did.

"For sure." Jelat nodded, trying to make out the landscape in the dark.

They went on foot from there. The house was farther than it appeared. Yanda scanned for sentient minds in the vicinity. She judged the place safe.

"There's a boy in the house thinking loud," Zami said to Yanda in mind-speak.

She checked. Yes, this time she did detect a curious mind, only partially shielded. "Oh, that's not good." Yanda connected with Ilan by mind and gave him this information.

"Thank you. I'll check on that." His eyes took on a laser focus. After a moment, he said, "I suspect you and Zami might have higher sense than most. The little boy is pretty well shielded but I'll mention it to the farm."

Yanda could see quite well at night. Without need of globe lights, which they decided to go without, she never stumbled as the big man Ilan next to her did, several times. Well, she thought, his feet were far below his eyes.

Night sounds arose as darkness increased — small

birds, crickets, and frogs set up a chorus after they passed. Larger animals moved in dry grasses.

And then they were on the front walk of the two-story farmhouse. At the door, they received a warm welcome by a cluster of adults and children eager to see new faces. Setoin had obviously communicated ahead.

To Yanda, it was strange to be so far from the parts of Alland familiar to her. She'd never been to Outer Alland and was fascinated by every detail: the scent and texture of the air, the minds of the people she was meeting. She also felt suddenly weary, registering what a long day it'd been. They'd started out at dawn, after all.

Their hosts seemed like simple country folk out of a storybook, at least in dress. But there was enough diversity among them that she could detect worldly personalities and troubled histories, as they talked around the dinner table.

After, sitting comfortably in the living room, a house cat jumped onto Yanda's lap. Zami, who loved every animal, had never seen a domestic cat. His hands went up to its furry neck as he established immediate rapport.

Ilan said gently in mind-speak to Yanda, "That's a powerful little aura your boy is building with the feline. He has a distinctive register. Does he know yet how to tune it low?"

Yanda felt a smack, like her mothering had been brought into question, but she only responded, "Let me see." She pressed her lips to Zami's curls, not because she was going to whisper but because physical contact formed the quietest direct communication between them. "Zami, Baby Button, make your feeling with kitty cat very, very small and quiet, okay? Like we do when we hide who we are."

In a fraction of a second, Ilan nodded. "Excellent. He

did it." Even in mind-speak, Yanda felt the emotion of the big red man as he admired her son's control, and her relationship with him. "Sentience trackers have a long reach," he mind-mumbled.

A woman named Canda, with a plain, friendly face said, "You must be tired after your day's journey. We settle early anyway, to rise with sun for farm work. I'll show you your rooms." Canda led the way upstairs to two guest rooms.

It was hard going through the motions of sheltering for the night when all she wanted was to get to where they were going. Though happy to take a break from the *swizzer*, every moment weighed on her.

"Can we use secure channels? I did that from the apartment in Skarth. Encrypted lines on my ENAC."

"You did what?" Jelat hissed with clenched teeth.

Ilan glanced up, brows furrowed.

"I could tell it was secure."

"I was on watch," Ilan said. "I would have detected if it wasn't."

"That won't be possible here," Setoin said from the doorway.

Yanda hadn't even known he was there. Something stirred in her belly with the revelation that he was listening in.

He entered, sat on a chair by the wall, and stretched out his legs, feet propped on a low table.

"What do you mean?" She'd planned on using her newfound skill with her ENAC 370, no matter what the others came up with. She wanted to hone the ability further.

Jelat sat on one of the beds, fiddling with a device.

"I suppose you're keeping that shielded," Setoin asked him.

"I'm not doing anything distant." The precocious-looking man set aside the device.

With her sight, Yanda looked beyond the walls, searching the air above and around the house. Ever since they'd detected the spy-bot, she'd been applying her farthest reach, which could travel across a city—it had, during her captivity in Dondar. She saw nothing to concern them.

Then she felt something wake in her laptop. She'd done nothing to make it happen, as far as she knew. Settling at the head of the narrow bed, with Zami sleeping against her, she closed her eyes to meditate. Mind shielded, as she'd been trained by Shouma, she sought the AI she'd detected the night before. For a brief moment, she was in the AI environment, and she knew no one in the room had detected. "Ha. Last time I say anything about this," she muttered to herself. But she set about making sure that signal was for her alone, using the encryption device that had taught her its access and use. Then she asked, "Wash up?"

"I'll show you." Setoin unfolded from his slouch and eased out of the room.

She left Zami sleeping and followed the rebel down the hall.

He pulled a towel from a closet next to the open bathroom door and handed it to her. Of average height, his brown eyes met hers with a warm sharing. Under a bandana, his hair bushed out, auburn. She tried to guess his age. With many talents, that was a hard thing to do. Thirties? Or of a slow-aging race?

She tried for a shower but the handles and pullies produced nothing. Reluctant to bother anyone, she ran tap water. "Maybe they're low water use," she thought, splashing the worst of the dust and bugs off her and slipping her nightgown over her head.

Once lights were turned out, the exhaustion evaporated and she thought she'd never sleep.

At some point, she must have drifted off because she woke having dreamed of her daughter on that other planet where they could only breathe from flowers.

Too sad from having felt Seiti in her dream, then lost her with waking, she got up quietly and went downstairs.

Outside, the air felt summery. She stood barefoot, looking across food-crop fields, dusted with a pre-dawn hint of light.

"Is your home much like this?"

She hadn't heard Setoin approach but he stood near her, gazing up at the stars.

"A lot like this, but not so far from the city." She gave a quiet chuckle, mostly a huff. "The whole planet's the same. No mountains, or forests, or oceans to mark any place as different."

"You've seen a lot of other worlds?" he asked.

"No. Only one other. And a moon where I was imprisoned in a dome. That's all there was on it—a cluster of domes, forever in shadow and black as night. You?"

"A few," he said, glancing at her, then back up at the slash of the solar system across the dark sky.

She studied his profile: hollowed cheeks, neat beard, pierced ear.

"You sound local," she said. "What's your story?"

# CHAPTER

# 10

S etoin responded, "We don't have long. We should leave while there's still a little dark. But I'm sure we'll have time to share our pasts."

As they walked back, Yanda asked, "Who made the tunnels?"

"Mining, I assume."

"Why did I never hear of these warrens while growing up here? The government must know about them. Why do you feel safe in them?" She was surprised at the questions bubbling.

"We keep watch." He glanced at her. "We know what government factions are up to."

"Are you so sure they're not aware of you?" she couldn't help asking.

"We're not so separate as you might think."

He sounded very tied in. It worried her. A whistle came, like a wood thrush. Setoin stood still under the eaves of the house. "Best get ready quickly," he said in mind-speak.

\* \* \*

Dressed for travel, they stood in the kitchen gulping down hot *kaffa*, and shoving rolls into their pockets to eat on the way. Zami, still half-asleep in his carrier, rested his head on Yanda's shoulder. She'd pulled on the hat to protect his ears from the morning cold, but also to hide their pointy shape.

Silently they filed down the path to the hidden *swizzers*. Ilan made a face as he stretched out on his.

"We should get close by late morning," Setoin assured him. "Though coordinates could change by the time we get there."

A small groan came from Ilan in answer.

They entered the tunnels and descended back into blackness just as first light hit the edges of the world.

\* \* \*

Unable to wait any longer, Yanda asked Setoin, "Are you getting any coordinates?"

It took a moment for the Allandian rebel to answer. Whizzing along ahead of her, he called, "I'm getting no read at all."

They shot into a sort of bowl, probably created by another meteor strike.

Climbing off his vehicle, Setoin said, "We're within range of where I left them." He stared at his device. He pulled various boosting instruments from his pockets and tried them.

Yanda wrung her hands and rubbed her eyes. Zami toddled off to explore. Yanda followed a pace behind; anything to move the adrenalin that spiked with nerves.

By afternoon, they moved into another tunnel. Setoin unfolded bedding and a meager supply of travelers' food from one of the hollowed-out storage nooks: dried, smoked fish, and fruit leathers, hard cheeses, water canteens—some packets of dried foods if they dared light a fire.

Yanda tried to tire Zami in a chase game. The men played as well. At last, they rolled into blankets and tried to sleep.

In the night, Yanda felt a tap in her mind.

"Can you make yourself invisible and silent?" It was Ilan.

"Zami can do that for both of us," she responded.

"Ask him."

Yanda spoke to her little boy, explaining what was needed. He swathed them in an undetectable sphere. Yanda picked up her satchel, their clothes bag, and Zami. Still dressed, she carried her boots, following Ilan's mind down a tunnel. When they'd gone a short way, they met up with Ilan, and she pulled on her boots.

"What's up?" she asked.

But he turned with a hand gesture to move on. He had to duck to miss the ceiling.

They did not speak until they'd climbed a steep incline, coming out onto a grassy verge.

She breathed deep of the open air, smelling of foliage warmed by early morning sun. "What's happened?" she asked again. She trusted Ilan but hated disconnecting with the others.

Ilan shook his head. "Let's keep walking. You need to completely shield."

"We're always shielding, but if we need to stay invisible, I can boost what Zami's doing so the little guy doesn't wear out."

"Good idea."

They walked a ways across bare land, staying among head-high bamboo-like plants, while Ilan read a handheld instrument. After a while, he led them into a tunnel.

"I feel like a rabbit," she said. "Down one hole, up another."

"*Tokong*. That's what we call them on Qontaq," Ilan said, and hopped.

Yanda and Zami grinned to see such a big man jump like a bunny.

She was too busy keeping them hidden to try to read his mind for duplicity. Anyway, he had formidable blocking abilities.

They navigated the tunnel, this one rougher than the others, until they came out into an underground space with multiple exits. "Let's sit here. I'll explain."

Yanda dropped against one curved wall, Zami snuggling onto her lap. She withdrew dried blueberries as a snack.

"I got a message. Setoin is not leading us toward the coordinates. Also, there are messages going from Jelat back to Skarth that shouldn't be happening."

"Do you think Jelat is messing with the readings? Blocking them from Setoin?"

"I suspect something like that." He gave her an approving glance. "I had coordinates yesterday. I told you that. They're not taking us there."

"Why didn't you say something?"

"Because I thought we'd better just get away. Others are coming for us. A faction I trust."

"Does Jelat know you have them?"

"Hopefully not, but he might guess. So, we have to

keep hidden from him and tell the rebels to move."

They sat a while in the dark tunnel, only a single float-globe lighting their faces.

Zami played in the space made by Yanda's stretched-out legs.

Yanda broke the silence. "So Jelat…what? He's been an enemy all along? In Pedore? In my apartment?"

"Seems maybe so. It's troubling."

"I'll say!" Yanda couldn't believe he'd use such a lightweight word for it. She looked around, cocking her head to listen. "Won't he find us? He's very clever." When Ilan didn't answer, she said, "Why couldn't he block them from you as he did from Setoin?"

Ilan adjusted his large frame to face Yanda. "I have some gifts with data. Besides those of obscuring. Jelat could not find the caves we're in if he tried. They are as if obliterated from the planet, for anyone except the fellow Qontaqians who are coming for us. One will take Jelat back to Skarth. The other two will lead Setoin, and us, to the refugee camp."

"I see." She sat with this new information, then said, "I think I understand gifts with data now. I wouldn't have a few days ago, but AI seems to be speaking to me, and I can sense when it's secure, like I can befriend it, into deep levels."

To Yanda's surprise, Ilan nodded. "I've sensed that part of your mind opening."

She gaped at him and began to protest but he stopped her, lifting a hand. "Don't be angry with me. I can't help myself. Even when I don't want to, I hear the minds around me. I can muffle them, but then I'm subduing my own thinking capacity." His eyes dropped fondly to Zami, who'd wiggled his bottom toward her so he could study Ilan, as if drawn like a moth to the man's emotions.

"I…I'm not angry. Exactly." She ducked her head in a silent chuckle. "I wonder, though, what you've spotted in me."

"I've come to see a sincere, deeply feeling woman. Honest, caring, self-sacrificing. Worried."

"Oh." She had no idea how to take so many compliments. She'd heard few in her life. Shouma was the first motherly figure who seemed to see her wholly and appreciate what she was. The Elves had mind-melded with her and still accepted her. But she was aware of profound cultural differences. She wasn't sure how fond they felt of her, if their interest in her centered on Zami. And the fact that she was Xentu.

"What brought you to Alland?" she asked now.

"It's a long story."

"They all are."

"How did you end up in captivity with two from my world?"

"You don't know that tale?" When he shook his head, she said, "I was captured, abducted from this planet. Ten of us were held captive. Krid collects those with gifts."

"I know only that Bonden was on Farn for a time, then brought to Terlond. That was not known in my home-world; there are those who would have gone after her. I learned it only once I was here, and by then, she'd escaped."

"She was captive with me on Farn and Terlond," Yanda verified. "She saved us. Brought us through many feet of stone to escape."

"It does not surprise. I've heard." His throat seemed

choked up as he spoke. Tears wet his eyes.

"I think she's been returned to your planet," Yanda hurried to say, hoping that would cheer him. But it didn't.

"No," he said with vehemence. "She should not go back. She was betrayed."

"I think the one who abducted her is prevented from his earlier evil doings. I hope so." She bent to nuzzle Zami's neck as he played with his hand-crafted animal. "My son is also in danger from Krid. I never know when he might look for him. If he's escaped from the Elves. He thinks he's his child."

"Is he the one who imprisoned Bonden?"

"Yes.

He shook his head at the massive hands folded in his lap. "It's hard to imagine anyone holding Bonden."

"Shouma told me she didn't want to leave without the rest of us. She's—" Yanda's throat tightened— "generous."

"That's how she's known." Ilan's eyes were intent on her face.

"Mage spies monitored us night and day, and Krid used powerful objects to control us. Maybe some affected her in particular. But when we got away to underground levels, she had her powers again."

"I need to warn Bonden," he said.

Just then they heard footsteps. A delicate androgynous person walked into the widened crossroads where several tunnels met.

Ilan held out a hand. "Sabra," he said with fond warmth. "How goes it?"

She put a hand in his massive one. "All good. Keelit and I absconded with a few *swizzers*. And we have e-bikes waiting for the last leg." Sabra bowed toward Yanda and

Zami. "This must be our precious cargo."

Ilan said, "Sabra, meet the surgeon and her Elf child."

"I'm honored." Sabra led the way.

# CHAPTER

# 11

**K**eelit was ordinary compared with his Qontaqian counterparts. Where Ilan and Sabra drew attention, one giantish, the other gnomish, Keelit resembled an accountant or bookkeeper. Pale hair, combed from the side, fell onto his forehead. He constantly pushed back one lock. His pasty complexion showed old acne scars. He bent his head down, shy, as they introduced themselves. Of average height—only slightly taller than Yanda—his shoulders slumped as he led the way.

They found the *swizzers*, mounted them and dipped deep into the earth in tunnels thick with blackness. Smells of dank earth grew fetid in places. Yanda longed for the surface and fresh air.

When at last they angled upward, Ilan let out a cry. He doubled over, rolled off the *swizzer*—which immediately dropped to the ground—and crouched.

Yanda shot to his side. "What's wrong?"

"A-attacked," Ilan managed to say through clenched teeth.

The other two Qontaqians held their heads in pain.

"Keelit, find a deeper passage." Ilan crossed his arms around his belly. "Jelat—I think. Someone's helping him. They're hunting us."

The plain young man—though age could be irrelevant—hunched against the tunnel wall, bent over an instrument. After a moment, he said, "Aradon got Jelat. I think he'll be able to subdue him. Sedon's bringing Setoin. I'll let them know the system we'll come through."

"You found something?" Ilan's red-gold hair flopped into his eyes, which were pressed shut as though he struggled against a gale force.

"Yeah." Keelit divulged no more but swept around a bend on his *swizzer*.

The rest hurried to catch up.

Yanda snuggled Zami under her arm. He lay at her side, holding on, eyes captivated by new places and adventures.

They aimed downward again into a tunnel only a few feet from floor to roof, the stones rough-cut, Yanda groaned internally. A drop from the dank ceiling fell in her eye and she shivered, sick of wet, sick of dark, sick of tight and rough and cold.

On his *swizzer* behind her, Ilan moaned occasionally, but the sound grew less agonized.

Yanda discovered an autopilot setting that kept them from hitting walls, for the most part preventing injury and taking some of the work out of flying so she could concentrate on holding Zami safely at her side. By the time they came to a sudden halt, her back ached incessantly.

"It doesn't go through." Keelit let his *swizzer* to the ground.

"We can't go back." Ilan's look of pain had finally eased. "Jelat may be captured but he was working with others. They'll know where we've been since I'm not shielding there anymore."

"I'm getting something from our friends." Keelit concentrated on his tiny handheld screen that lit his face in pale contours. "We have to leave the swizzers." He got off his now-inert flyer and groped along the wall, head-lamp aimed at solid rock.

The rest stretched their muscles and watched him, waiting.

Yanda bounced Zami who struggled, wanting to get down and explore. "Not yet, sweetie."

"I got it." Keelit peered into a narrow gap as they crowded behind him.

"I can't fit in there," Ilan said with horror.

Yanda held Zami's gaze a moment, then said, "Zam can make you into something smaller."

"Like, make *me* smaller?" Ilan asked.

"A rabbit." Zami suggested with an impish expression.

Yanda remembered the incongruous hop the large man had managed, to their delight, and chuckled.

"Oh, no, I don't think—" Suddenly a small gray rabbit was sniffing the ground at their feet.

"Oh jeez," Keelit said, staring.

Sabra held her waist and bent forward laughing. "He's going to be so mad."

"I might prefer to go as a bunny as well," Yanda said, "but I'm okay." She didn't want to lose hold of Zami.

The rest could squeeze through. Sabra picked up Ilan in bunny form. He struggled, but she held on, petting his head. His eyes grew wide. Small animal thoughts came into Yanda's mind, incomprehensible for the most part, though there were fleeting images of her son, the way a rabbit might see him. This was interesting. But she was occupied with getting herself and Zami through the narrow crack between rocks as he held Ilan's small form with his mind. She worried what could happen if Zami tired and the man took his full shape again between the tight crags.

She heard loud rumbling ahead, and with one last squeeze, tumbled out into an underground cavern with a subterranean river feeding into a pool. A waterfall plummeted thirty feet, filling the air with pounding vibrations.

"Make Ilan into his big man form again," Yanda whispered to Zami.

He did, and clapped at his success.

Ilan twisted from side to side and touched his body. Then he eyed the little Elf child in Yanda's arms and lowered his head like a bull ready to charge. But all he did was slip immense hands onto Zami's soft cheeks and nod. "Talented."

Zami hooked his hands on Ilan's fingers and grinned up into the man's face. For a second, Yanda sensed a mind-exchange between them and Ilan's brows shot up and down. He patted the toddler's shoulders gently, as if he were releasing a bird into nature, seeming to keep his colossal strength in check with conscious will. Then he turned and Yanda saw several two-legged creatures skirting the lake, headlamps bobbing. Ilan waved. The parties met in the middle where a cave mouth mawed, large and easily traveled, behind the falls.

Introductions scooted through Yanda's exhausted mind like a fine mist.

Their climb out of the lake cavern became a blur in Yanda's memory. Others helped with Zami as she trudged, one foot after the other, satchel and cloth bag draping from her sagging shoulders. Later, she mainly recalled emerging into sunlight, leaving dark, dank scents behind. A breeze played with the feather-light fronds of miniature trees, only head-height, that hid eight bikes. She smelled wild grasses. It could as well be a field near Balyou from her childhood, yet they were very far now from there, from anywhere she'd ever been on her planet.

The electric two-wheelers mostly floated but could go on wheels. Yanda sat Zami in front of her. She only had to touch the controls and a diagram appeared in her mind. She wondered if this was a feature added by engineers with psi. The thought of technologies designed by and for those with talents like hers sent a frisson of excitement through her.

Silently, they moved single-file along narrow, little-used paths.

"The camp is on the move," came an unfamiliar mind-register. One of the newcomers. "We'll be able to meet up sometime tonight. I imagine you're hungry and tired."

She answered in the affirmative, wondering if he'd asked everyone or just her. Then she caught his name. Kelef.

"We need to keep going for a while to get completely out of range and scrub where we've been, but we will rest and eat. I promise."

What Yanda remembered later was the sight of the caravan crossing a bridge on a road joining theirs. Twenty tiny homes floating quietly on their forcefield pads progressed across the span and approached them. They descended into a crater—the third she'd seen since her re-turn to the planet of her childhood—and circled inside. Yanda and her party biked down the ramp and settled their *sedpods* to one side.

Zami struggled to the ground. Yanda let him go, trailing behind him as he ran toward a caravan that had just lowered to the ground. Its outer walls were painted with nature scenes. The door—salmon-colored with gold-trim—flew open and a round-faced woman stepped out. Several animals ran toward Zami as he barreled in their direction. A marsupial leaped onto his arm and climbed onto his shoulder, nuzzling his neck. He scooped the others into his arms: a baby bunny, a duck, and a bird with an injured wing that fluttered onto his knee as he crouched.

The camp—rebels, they were called, though in fact they were all ages and demeanors, and looked like any-one she'd meet on the street—stepped from their mobile homes and gathered near her, gazing at the Elf boy who clearly drew the animals to him.

The woman with the cherubic face knelt by him. "I'm Andle." She stroked the duck who quacked incessantly. "They like you."

Yanda hadn't asked him to make his eyes not swirl, or his ears mimic those of non-Elves; they would need to know her son for who he was, as they all had vulnerabil-ities.

Yanda thought she detected a protective cover, maybe an obscuring electrical grid, moved across over their heads, leaving the sunset colors deepening in the sky still visible. Yanda surmised that, from above, that is, if a drone were flying over, it would look like a field of grass, like at Pedore.

Where the screen dipped to meet the road, two new figures walked through, a row of lights signaling they'd entered using a code. Yanda recognized Setoin. The other must be the Qontaqian, Sedon.

Setoin spotted her and approached, hesitant, lifting his arms as though he might welcome an embrace.

She glanced at his face, then dropped her eyes. Tears pricked. She'd trusted him. They'd shared a bonding moment. Now she couldn't know how much he'd colluded with Jelat.

"It wasn't me," Setoin said, quietly. "I thought Jelat was…with us." He seemed choked up. His eyes darted to the rest, both hopeful and contrite.

Ilan slapped his shoulder with his mitt-sized hand, making Setoin fall forward before he caught himself. "I know you were hoodwinked. Come on. We're gonna start dinner."

Yanda hoped Ilan was right.

Three cylinders the size of car wheels floated in a cluster from one of the larger caravans. They seemed to heat up without visible power. Roasting veggies and breaded fish soon sent waves of delectable aromas.

When tables were laid out and set, she and Zami settled, excited to dig into a full plate.

Andle sat by them. Middle-aged by appearance, her stature was both muscly and soft at the same time.

"Are you a vet?" Yanda asked, indicating the animal still perching on her son's shoulder.

"Used to be a scientist," Andle said.

"Then I'm sure you still are." Yanda examined a charred object on her plate.

"Now I rescue things." Andle chuckled and brought a *sadi snip* to her mouth, blowing.

Setoin stood across from them, checking with Yanda first.

She flipped up a palm, inviting him.

He dropped to the bench attached to the foldout table. "You can stay in my home." He pointed behind at a bright turquoise-and-purple caravan. "I can stay with Zebel."

Mouth half-full, Yanda said, "I thought you guys would camouflage more on the road. That's pretty bright."

"It doesn't matter. We're always shielded anyway." He dipped a fried catatuga-puppy in sauce and popped it in his mouth, chewing delightedly.

Zami still had the little marsupial by his neck though Andle had shut the rest away. "I feed it?" he asked.

"Nic-nic," Andle said. "She's a woo-loo. Native to this outback. How about a little of the *sadi snip*?" She held out a pale melon-orange slice.

Zami's eyes brightened and he scooped the bitty creature into his hand. Holding her to his chest, he gave her the sauteed vegetable and watched as Nic-nic grasped it in miniscule hands, nibbling. He grinned up at Yanda and she smiled back.

After supper, Setoin showed them his compact home, pointed out the amenities, and left them to settle in.

# Part II

# CHAPTER

# 12

**On Planet Terlond**
**Mnenu**

Mnenu sat at the desk of the Voice of Ash-don, a post his mother had held before him. Some strange quality of mind allowed them to endure the blast of Ash-don's energy—a mind-force capable of powering the city and holding knowledge of the universe—and soften it for the Circle, the strongest other sentients among the Neyla elves. In the year he'd acted in this role, he'd learned a lot about himself. He'd also lost freedom.

He shoved from the ornately carved desk and crossed to the windows. Sea water pressed to the glassine—a powerful transparent material the elves made in their undersea mountain world, by grinding and heating, with the use of kelp extracts. The sealant they made kept out all water so their tall bookshelves remained dry.

Gazing into the sea, he watched a sea horse float by. Farther off, a *tesu* swam toward the surface high above, then shot out of the water, leaping.

He couldn't bear it. "I'm taking a break," he said into a wrist device, and burst out of the office, to make his way to the deep recesses of the sea.

## On Alland
## Yanda

For a month, Yanda cobbled together a life for her and her half-elf toddler, Zami, in rebel camps on her home planet of Alland. These were good folk; their only "crime" was to have powerful abilities, like her ability to read minds and see through walls. She'd come seeking her daughter, whem she'd been told went to the rebels of Outer Alland.

Now Yanda applied her medical skills to help the rebels as she waited for their advanced tech to locate her daughter. But they were coming up with nothing.

One evening, as she sat by her cook fire talking with a few compatriots of the rebel camp, a seven-foot Elf, orange cockatiel-hair peaked in a mohawk, strode toward them. Merne, also captivating, followed behind, her hair, brown and green like lichen, twined in tendrils around her face, her ears like long pointed leaves. At the sight of the two tall female elves, Yanda leapt up with a cry. Could this be? Tlalit and Merne—partners, shifters, high members of the forest elf clan of Terlond—were here on her planet, Alland? Yanda threw her arms around one, then the other, laughing, crying.

At last, sobering, she asked, "How did you find me?"

# MARIE JUDSON

## On Planet Terlond
## Mnenu

Mnenu scanned the surface of the sea, then dove, covering great distances with his long strokes, his body now that of a sea creature. *Lanten*, they called that state. In this transformed body, his senses took in the sea as a scent and a taste. He felt all sentient life around him, opened up to the waters, listening with his skin as well as his mind. He headed for his favorite caves, at the base of their sea mountain home, Zotoul.

## Yanda

Seeing her elven friends brought a mix of emotions to Yanda, joy but also fear, that if they could detect the camp's location, others could, too. They might have given the rebel location away. "Sit. I'll introduce you," Yanda said. "Andle, Sandor, Kelef, meet my dear friends from Terlond. They helped save us from Krid."

"Zami!" Merne threw her arms open as the little boy ran to his mama trailing several small animals, including a duck.

Yanda scooped him up. Firelight flickered over his caramel skin. He had the swirling eyes of the elves, his iridescent blue with flecks of orange and green. Leaf-point ears nestled in curls of burnished red-brown hair, magenta at the tips.

Merne looked disappointed. She'd grown close to Zami on Terlond but that was months ago.

"Good to meet you." Tlalit bowed toward those sitting around the fire. Jewels along one pointed ear twinkled in the firelight with her movement. Once she'd sat in the proferred chair, she turned to Yanda. "You know I can find anyone anywhere." She smiled, consommately confident. "Of course we completely shielded to land."

"I figured," Yanda placated. But still. "Where's your ship?"

## Mnenu

On Terlond, the sea elf, Mnenu, called to his favorite *tesu*, Te-Weet, with his mind. Seconds later, the dolphin-like creature, a luminous shade of aquamarine, descended toward him. Mnenu was a strong swimmer and could cover miles under the sea but for reaching the lower caves and navigating tunnels, Te-Weet was a great help, and sleeker than him.

Mnenu caught Te-Weet's dorsal fin as the *tesu* shot past. All it took was a mental image of where he wanted to go and Te-Weet aimed there.

Sharing the sea with the cetacean was one of Mnenu's favorite aspects of life: seeing, feeling, smelling the way Te-Weet did. It was an alternate reality. Te-Weet's mind was a happy place, without fear or worry, for the most part.

## Yanda

Yanda poked the fire with bamboo, head cocked for Tlalit's answer. The others listened avidly as well.

"The Sarsefi is not far," Tlalit said.

The planet of Alland had no trees, only bushes and relatively low-growing foliage. Cut through by natural canals, the planet had no seas or large bodies of water. It was not easy to hide things. Yanda tried to imagine how the elf had brought the ship into Alland's atmospher, and to their countryside location without being noticed. Could she cloak that well? Alland was known for sophisticated surveillance.

Merne reached again to Zami for a hug but he snuggled into Yanda and studied Merne from that distance.

Scooting her chair closer to Yanda, Merne leaned toward them. "Little brother." She touched the boy's forehead with hers in the Elven greeting.

Yanda felt their brief mind-meld, though it did not include her. That always bothered her, when others connected with her son and kept her out. She turned to Tlalit. "I heard you bought a ship and offered to deliver our friends to their planets. That was nice. Did they all make it home?"

"Some," Tlalit said.

"You're a star captain now." Yanda grinned. It didn't surprise her in the least. Tlalit was brilliant with networks, controls, programming.

"But we came here with news," Merne said.

## Mnenu

On Terlond, Mnenu shot through subterranean channels, climbed, scrambled, until he reached the steaming pool in hollowed-out stone at the back of a dark cavern, his favorite place to think. Sinking deep, he breathed in the rich smells of rock and phosphorescent lichens that glowed in an array of hues. He shut his eyes, closing out the sounds of bathers in the outer chambers with pools of varying temperatures.

He had a lot to think about. With his brother's death, he was now the voice of Ash-don. He'd had to return home from the university on Tusca's moon where he'd planned to finish his graduate degree, then travel farther into the universe.

I love my Neyla clan. But am I willing to sacrifice myself to remain the voice of the Stone? His freedom seemed gone as he served as priest in the Stone's massive sea-cave chamber.

## Yanda

News, for me? Possibilities shot through her mind, pinging like a pinball. Had Zamani sent them to take back their son? Was it about Tenali, Zamani's grandson, Merne's son, Yanda's sometime-lover? Kridenit hadn't escaped, had he? She froze at the thought that he might even now be on her trail.

"A girl was spotted in Blenin, on Shagal. That's a—" Tlalit started to explain the location.

Yanda interrupted, "I know, Shagal's a moon in a nearby star system." She gripped her hands in her lap, not daring to hope. "A girl?"

Tlalit flipped out a hand-held and showed Yanda a blurred vid caught on closed-circuit surveillance camera. Faintly, one could make out a child, maybe eight, slipping past on a dirty city street.

Yanda squinted, trying to discern if it could be her daughter. She knew Blenin was rough, diverse hub of trade routes and crime. She hugged Zami and rocked, taking quick shallow breaths. "When was this caught?" Yanda barely squeezed out the words.

"Weeks ago. You know it takes a while to reach Alland from Terlond, and we didn't know how to communicate with you."

"Yet you found me." Yanda let that hang in the air. "Who sent it to you?"

Merne and Tlalit exchanged a glance. "Tenali asked us to look into it."

"You've been in touch with him?" Yanda's heart beat wildly, though she tried to hide how much she was affected by this. She gripped Zami so hard, he shifted with a protest. She stroked his arm, adjusting him in her lap and kissing his cheek. He still stared at Merne and Tlalit, maybe piecing together memories from his early months. "Can you take me there? I'll gather a few things." Yanda made ready to stand.

"Hold on. We can't leave tonight." Merne squeezed Yanda's knee. "Besides, there have been no more sightings of the girl on Shagal."

"No more sightings." Yanda's throat tightened, emotion threatening to overwhelm her. She sat silent, looking through tears from one elf to the other.

## Mnenu

On Terlond, Mnenu found himself going back over his brother's death. Everyone said it was not his fault. But was that true? Edon had been the subdued, level-headed older brother, leaving Mnenu to his wild life, short bursts of study, long stretches of going *lanten* and swimming with the *tesu*. He'd disappear on his boat for weeks, take lovers and as easily drop them, while Edon stayed, the loyal son, studying the ancient lore of the Neyla, and the discipline of mind necessary to sit in the Circle of the Stone.

On one of Mnenu's visits home from university, Edon had asked a trip on Mnenu's boat.

Mnenu said, "Take it then." He had other plans that day.

The boat had been found, abandoned. Edon had never been found.

"He would not desert us," his parents insisted, broken hearted. But Edon was mourned, a ceremony of the Great Return performed.

And Mnenu was named the new Voice. The job had passed down through generations of the family for a thousand years.

## Yanda

"What do you suggest?" Yanda asked, controlling her urge to thrash out into the universe after her daughter.

"The Great Stones on Terlond have the farthest reach. You could ask Shalt to search for a mind-register similar to yours, with the Circle's help," Merne suggested.

"I should have done that in the first place. Never left Terlond." Yanda hitched a sob. All these months wasted.

Zami twisted around and stared at his mother with worried eyes.

"It's okay, Button. Don't worry." She wiped her face and gave him a smile.

"You didn't know," Tlalit said. "You assumed she was here, at your home, with your parents."

"What about the Stone of the Neyla?" Yanda asked. She felt if Shalt knew, she would have gotten the message from him when they were completely in synch, her helping to pull the Stone's pieces from across the universe.

Merne frowned. "Why Ash-don, not Shalt?"

"I don't...I don't really want to go back to that area just yet," Yanda said, feeling cornered. "Isn't Krid still there, imprisoned in the caves behind the Stone?"

"No, he was allowed to return to Farn, his moon."

Yanda's mouth dropped open as acid ran through her veins. "Allowed to...what do you mean?" She couldn't believe they'd let him go free, a mage of his cruelty, who abducted anyone or anything of power for his collection. He'd stolen years of her life, kept her and her son prisoner, along with the other fems in captivity with them.

Merne tried to assure her, "His mansion in Dondar was confiscated. We've put tags on him. Tenali has refused to give him transport so he's reliant on public means of travel. And he's monitored at all times. We also want to catch whoever helped him."

Yanda let out a huff of air. "You think that's enough? And why should he be free?"

"What entity is going to imprison him? He imprisons. We do not."

Yanda felt sick. She'd been sure he would no longer be a threat. Zami rested against her chest. She took comfort in the warm weight of him. "I think I need to get this boy to bed. You can stay with us," she offered the elves. "I'll sleep outside. It's warm enough."

"We secured accommodation online." Tlalit stood, towering over them.

"You what?"

Tlalit laughed. "In one of the other wagons in your caravan. A sort of B&B."

"What the heck? Someone advertised their..." Yanda stared, flabbergasted, looking around at the others in her group who'd remained silent, expressions ranging from fascinated to horrified. "You do realize these people are on the run?"

"Don't worry," Tlalit said, calmly. "It's an underground web. Fully encrypted."

"That's not real comforting. But..." Yanda stood, lifting her boy. "Which one?"

They pointed down the row.

"Purple and turquoise," Tlalit said.

"Ah. Setoin's. He goes to Batan each year for the healing waters." He'd turned out to be a good friend, though Yanda had never entirely trusted him since his seeming duplicity on their journey to the rebel camps.

"It's a charming wagon," Merne said, smiling with gladness that they were in less explosive conversational territory.

"You've already been to it?" Yanda had qualms. "How long?"

"We just put our things there before coming here to your fire," Tlalit hurried to explain.

Yanda felt the slightest tremor of prevarication. Had Tlalit and Merne been watching her before they came to say hello? If so, why?

The others got up as well, mumbling "nice to meet you," eyes still wary.

Andle squeezed Zami's hand. "Sleep well, little one."

She and the other rebels melted into the night.

Tlalit said, "Let's talk in the morning. We'll form a plan." She and Merne glanced at each other, something dark lurking behind their eyes.

Red flags shot up in Yanda's already tense mind. "Wait, just let me put him to bed." She climbed the steps to her tiny movable house, laid Zami in his bed, and kissed him. "I'll be right back."

Outside, she asked the elves, "What's wrong?"

"It's just...something we didn't say. A *Blaz* trader was

docked at the time the photo was grabbed. It left soon after."

Bile rose as Merne's words registered; her daughter may have been captured by Blaz traders: traffickers, slavers, torturers. Yanda leaned against her trailer. "Shit, shit, shit. No, no, no, no, no."

Her mental cry went out across the universe, all the way  to Terlond where Zamani heard it in his treehouse. The massive Stone, Shalt, shook in response to her outburst of emotion. A ripple ran through the Circle of powerful mind-workers sitting on the great stone seats in the Crystal Pyramid called Vashal.

# CHAPTER

# 13

## Mnenu

The surface of the water around Mnenu, the sea elf, shivered and rippled as an immense, mournful shout throbbed in his head. He dug his palms into his temples, eyes wide. Voices from the pools below raised in confusion.

What could make such a sound? It was not on this planet. He knew that. It was out there, somewhere in the universe. Something in the profound aching cry sent an aching response in his belly. He thought he'd never lose the agony of it; it seared his soul.

Mnenu left the pool, knowing the Circle of Ash-don would meet.

## Yanda

Tlalit and Merne wrapped their arms around Yanda, pouring

healing sympathy into her in the way of the elves.

Merne murmured, "There's no confirmation that she was on that ship, or that it was even her in that image," to comfort Yanda before she shook both planets again.

Yanda nodded. She heard a sleepy question from Zami in her mind, from where he lay in bed. "What's wrong, mama?"

"It's okay. All is well. We're safe," she thought back to him.

With lingering trepidation, she said good-night and watched Merne and Tlalit walk away hand-in-hand down the track wide enough for their wagons and not much more.

## Mnenu

Mnenu climbed to his high stone seat in the circle of stone seats around the thirty-foot hole. Ocean could be heard crashing below where the Great Stone, Ash-don, pushed up through the surface of the water. As the mind-meld formed among the twelve Neyla who sat in the circle, Ash-don's powerful energy joined them.

There had been a rift between the sea elves and the forest elves for nearly a century, since the Neyna's forest home had been invaded by colonists. At first they'd come peacefully. But then, sensing the Neyna's power source, Shalt, the great stone that helped them tap elemental energies, they had attacked Ash-don's brother stone, blowing out pieces to sell or keep on other planets and moons across the universe. With its perfect sphere marred, Shalt had suffered, and so had the elves.

Fearing a similar fate, the Neyla cut ties with their forest cousins. They felt the Neyna elves could have prevented this, deterred the colonists more effectively. That they should have fought the invasion rather than welcoming them. That they should leave their home on the continent they shared with the human city of Dondar.

Zamani, leader of the Neyna, and the Circle on Vashal had tried to draw the fragments back from across the universe. Failing they called for other help, and Yanda had come. She had the resonance, with the help of all the powerful fems who'd been gathered by Krid, and at last the Circle of Ash-don helped as well. Ironically, though Krid had collected fems with reknowned special skills for his own power, in the end he'd created a team that could defeat him, restore Shalt to wholeness, and mend the rift between the Elven clans.

Now Shalt called to Ash-don announcing that the cry had been made by none other than Yanda, the part-Xentu who'd brought Shalt to wholeness. Yanda.

Mnenu gripped the arms of his chair. He'd met Yanda. She'd been on his boat last Withum.

## Yanda

When morning light hit Yanda's bedroom, she heard Zami's voice outside, shouting, reveling in life. Sitting up, she looked out the window and saw him at Andle's, playing with the animals.

Andle adored Zami. They had a special bond. The middle-aged woman, with hair like orange candy floss puffed around her head, had built her cottage on wheels. She's been a vet in her life before becoming a refugee.

Yanda gulped a sob as she came out on the stoop. Zami ran to her, the baby marsupial, NikNik, on his shoulder. She scooped him up. How could she leave him?

But how could she not? He'd be cared for here. Where might she end up? On Blaz, a planet of enslavers and torturers? "I'll go find Seiti and come back," she said to herself, nuzzling his sweet neck.

## Mnenu

"What is her trouble?" Mnenu shared in mind-speak with the Circle and two Great Stones. He felt the Neyna circle join theirs. From Alland, Tlalit and Merne tapped in.

Zamani, in the Neyna circle, knew. "She seeks her missing daughter, who left her home planet in search of her mother. The girl is only eight in Alland years, though she has Xentu blood."

Merne added, "We've spotted a girl in Blenin but it's unclear if it's her. At the time of the sighting, Blaz traders were in the vicinity. It was when we shared that with Yanda that she let loose that cry."

Mnenu thought, *That was clumsy.* But to the Circles and Stones, he said, "How might we help?"

## Yanda

Yanda set Zami down. As he ran off, Tlalit and Merne arrived. Yanda asked them, "Will we go to Shagal, try to find out if Seiti was there? Follow her trail? Or you could just take me there. Leave me to follow her."

The elves looked skeptical.

She added, "I have funds. I'll bring photos and ask around."

"Alone?" Merne frowned. "Look, Yanda, better we get Shalt's help. At this point, no time should be lost. The Circle can search Blaz, make sure—"

Yanda interrupted, "I don't want to go to the Neyna. I'd like to speak with the other circle. With the Neyla stone. Ash-don has called to me recently."

Tlalit and Merne frowned deeply.

"Why?" Merne asked.

Yanda owed her. After all, the talented Merne had metamorphosed into an old woman and hidden herself for a year in the toxic slums of Sheffed, gaining allies among the mage spies and setting up the fems' escape.

The two Elves studied Yanda, obviously hurt that she chose the Neyla over the Neyna for help.

Yanda swallowed, her face closed in a stubborn glaze. She couldn't tell them she feared losing her son to Zamani, Merne's father.

Merne took her hand. "My son, Tenali, has ties with the Neyla, but we do not. We can't land our ship there. We can land at Dondar. Then, if you wish, you can travel to the Neyla. Or connect with them from our Circle. It's much safer. And would have twice the power."

Yanda squeezed Merne's hand back but remained silent and closed off.

Merne hurried on, "Dondar is much cleaner now. The air is *tzak*." Clean, in Elven speak. "And with Krid gone from Terlond…"

Yanda searched within herself and had to admit that, besides her other objections, returning to Shalt scared her: melding with the Great Stone, helping to pull its pieces from across the universe, had been shattering. She thought she'd lose her mind in the process. It'd taken months to recover. Besides, shouldn't the Stone have known her daughter had left her home planet seeking Yanda? If not then, could Shalt sense more now? Tenali had said Ash-don was just as powerful, or more so. What would it be like to approach the twin power stone? Would it be less jarring?

"You'll drop me by the Neyla," Yanda said with finality. "You needn't land. Just get me close."

"But ... do you swim?" Tlalit asked, knowing this planet Yanda grew up on had no seas at all. "You'll be in the middle of the ocean."

\* \* \*

Yanda bobbed on sea waves, terrified, despite the lifesaver ring Tlalit had given her before letting her down onto the surface of Terlondian sea and flown away before the Neyla detected them. Though she'd learned to float and swim a little in swimming pools, and the natural pools of Rotoul, this vast, bottomless water petrified her. She didn't think it would. She'd gone there in spirit travel with Zamani, and again with Tenali and it felt safe.

Now, who knew what creatures might be swimming under her?

Yanda wished—not for the first time—that she'd thought the drop off through a bit better. Even more, she wished she could take on this mission with her team of escapees: Shouma, who could read minds and influence anyone, near or far, who could disappear and appear, jump across space; Bonden, who invented devices and could move through walls; and especially Vatu, part amphibian, shapeshifter, who'd grown up on a planet that was all ocean. Where was her Mingalian friend now?

She clung to the inflatable, trying to keep salty brine from going up her nose and down her throat, as waves hit her from one side, then another. All was blackness, the only sound the endless lapping of water surrounding her.

Tlalit had wanted the obscuring of night and put her ship to float silently, cloaked, undetectable, but still. Yanda assured her it'd be fine.

Why had she chosen this particular approach? She asked herself with rising panic as she pumped her legs futilely, trying to sense her location. Wasn't she supposed to be good at that, from her training with Shouma? Something bumped against her and she jerked away, gasping, heart hammering.

Gentle thoughts filled her head. *Not danger*, a *tesu* transmitted to her.

She remembered the feel of the sentient sea creatures from her boat-trip with the Neyla the year before. More *tesu* gathered around her, chirruping.

"You're tired," one said, and bumped its head under her arm.

Tentatively, Yanda wrapped her arm around its cool rubbery exterior, then, with growing confidence, hugged it. "A bit," she admitted, spitting out ocean water that was becoming harsh in her throat.

"I am Te-weet," the creature told her. The *tesu* bumped her until she pulled onto its back, gripping the dorsal fin.

Yanda laughed with joy as they shot across the water, the tesu's blow hole spouting splats of spray into her face. "I have to bring Zami to do this," she thought, feeling less alone, more in equilibrium with the vast sea that spread in all directions.

"I take you to boats," Te-weet said.

Boats? This wasn't exactly what she'd imagined. But what *had* she pictured? Tenali had told her some of the city was held in place by huge kelp roots. She recalled his mouth on hers, giving her oxygen, as they plummeted downward together. Her heart raced with the memory. How would she enter the city without him?

But he'd left her. Dropped her off on Alland and deserted her, without a word. Why? She'd thought he cared about her and Zami, his half-brother.

The pod of *tesu* swam and leapt with her on Te-Weet's back. Cloud cover moved away and a violet moon revealed an atoll where several boats bobbed, cresting waves. The rigs were covered in carvings like the one she'd been on going to the Withum festival.

"Can you climb up?" Te-Weet asked, hovering in place with its powerful tail.

There was no ladder in sight. Why hadn't she gotten lessons in teleporting from Bonden or Dele? Maybe she couldn't learn it. Holding Te-weet tight around the neck, she used her sight to peer through the side of the boat and spotted a strong rope ladder coiled on the deck. But how could she move it?

Think! She berated herself. She could move obstructions in a person's body in surgery. But that was tiny bits of congestion, or blood clots, not a heavy bundle of rope. Gripping her hands together, she willed the rope to rise and felt minds helping her. The hemp budged incrementally. She took a quick breath and, elated. tried again.

"I see in your head you move ladder. You fine witch human," Te-weet extolled her efforts. "Get it higher. Kala jump, grab."

Yanda rolled her head, loosening tight muscles. Then, arms gripped to the *tesu* and drawing strength from it, she set her sight again on the rope and, breathing long, slow breaths, put her will into raising the coil. She saw it rise above the edge of the boat. Quick as lightning, a *tesu* the opalescent hue of a pale moon shot into the air, nipped, and tugged hard, yanking backward with a push off the gunwale. The ladder dropped down the outer boatside. Te-weet swam close and Yanda grabbed, stepping onto the lowest rung. Letting the tesu go, she swung with a thud against the wood siding. Pulling with all her might, she lifted her wet weight to the next step, then climbed. "Note to self. More climbing exercises in routines, when I'm back at the rebel camp."

Incrementally, Yanda made her way to the top. Reaching over, she found a place to grip and hauled herself over the rim, then flung a leg up and over. *Not impressive agility*, she thought, as six *tesu* watched, heads bobbing in the water below.

Climbing on deck, she wondered, "What next? Wait for someone to decide to take a boat out for an excursion?? It seemed like the middle of the night, though she thought Tlalit had said it was close to dawn. She'd been too jittery to listen properly. She tried to remember the moons of Terlond. What did it mean when the violet one hovered above?

"We tell Neyla," Te-weet called to her.

"Thank you!" she called. What if they hadn't come along? She couldn't imagine. Wouldn't try.

What was she doing here? The only Neyla she'd gotten to know at all had infuriated her; frankly, she hoped never to see Mnenu again after he'd knocked her off the boat and dragged her under water with him, thinking…whatever he was thinking. That was her first time in deep water. He'd been so arrogant. Given no apology.

Maybe he'd moved away, left the planet. Hadn't she heard he went to do a graduate degree on a moon somewhere.

She crouched out of the breeze, hugged herself, teeth

chattering. The tesu had been kind to her. Were they so kind to everyone who jumped into their waters? She wished she at least had Mnenu's way of drying instantly by a mere touch of his hands. She looked around the boatdeck, wondering where she might sleep. Maybe she should pull the rope back up.

This was seeming like an absurd idea now. The Neyla didn't know her. In fact, they and the Neyna were in some ways enemies. And she was tied to the forest Elves through her son, and his father. The two Power Circles helping to pull Shalt's pieces together, keeping Kridenit's attacks at bay, was their first and only cooperation in a very long time.

Suddenly an Elven head popped into sight above the boat's side. Startled, Yanda jumped away. With ease, a tall sea elf stepped over the side. She was lovely, etched in lavender moonlight. Tiny seashells outlined her face, embedded in her skin.

"I'm Malu." The female sea elf came forward and pressed her forehead to Yanda's, giving a light mindtouch. "I remember you from the Withum Festival last year. You're cold. Here." Her hands, touching Yanda's shoulders, instantly dried her, even her hair.

"I'm sorry I didn't recognize you." Yanda apologized for backing away. "Thank you for drying me." Her teeth's chattering had slowed. "But I guess we'll just get wet again." She had stood and now looked reticently at the choppy waves. She wiped snot and seawater from under her nose. *Jeez. Why can't I be cool like this pillar of Elven grace?*

"It will be better if you learn to transform to *lanten*." Malu disappeared into a small cabin on the deck.

"*Lanten*?" Yanda asked, following.

Malu came out holding a head-shaped hood attached to a tube and large gourd shape. She held it out.

It reminded Yanda of the breathing apparatus Bonden had invented for Vatu, to keep out the toxic air of Dondar. She slipped it over her head, panicking briefly as it sealed around her face, like seaweed drying. Quickly she adjusted the tube over her nose, slipping the straps over her shoulders, and breathed in. Fresh air came from the bulb that now pressed into her back.

"Here we go." Malu picked her up and jumped over the side.

Yanda gasped as they sank, Malu pulling her downward. Despite Yanda's efforts to stay calm, she felt panic, and made herself inhale and exhale as they plunged deeper into black waters.

Te-weet and the other *tesu* swam around them them but soon became small dots on the surface above. Yanda sent another mental thanks to them.

Slowly she gained some confidence that she wouldn't drown as Malu swam on, pulling. Yanda kicked her feeble, human feet, filling her lungs from the tube. After a while, she made out lights in the watery depths. They drew closer, and she spotted balls glowing in dark arches. A sort of castle took form, descending out of sight into the depths. How else to describe it, with its towers and turrets? Like in storybooks she'd read with Seiti.

Yanda's muscles ached by the time they landed on a rock shelf on the side of a cliff, even though she'd done little of the work. The castle-like structure was no longer visible. Yanda saw only what appeared to be an underwater mountainside.

Malu created a glow-globe to float in front of them as they entered a tunnel. They navigated several before they stopped at a rubber-like covering which they pushed through. They crossed a series of chambers. The last was dry, glowing with heat bulbs. Yanda heard the surf shushing and pounding against rocks out of sight. There was a bed, and a desk, even carpets and woven wall hangings.

"Can I take this off?" Yanda asked in a muffled voice, scrabbling her fingers under the seal at her neck.

"Here." Malu tucked her fingertips beneath the edge and it loosened.

Yanda gasped with relief as Malu dragged the hood off her head.

"Tenali stayed here when he first came to us," Malu said.

Hearing the name, Yanda tensed, the familiar ache rushing into her belly, then her heart: *he deserted me*.

"I hope you'll be comfortable in here," Malu said. "Oxygen is vented in. I'll bring you food."

After Malu left, Yanda had to wonder, was she a prisoner?

# CHAPTER

# 14

**Mnenu**

Menu climbed into bed with a book. Darkness above him was animated by the quiet murmur of water on glass. When away from his sea home, he missed that sound.

Malu mind-spoke to him. "She's here."

Mnenu set the book aside, fighting the urge to leap out of bed and go find Yanda.

"Where have you put her?"

"Our guest chamber."

"The Bloob." Mnenu grimaced.How does she…is she fine?"

"Well, she needs a dry oxygenated room. She's human."

Somewhat, he thought. They both knew what she could do. She'd helped piece Shalt, the other Great Stone, back together. And recently mind-shouted so loud, a large portion of the universe must have heard. "Thank you for getting her," he said, closing their mind connection.

He hadn't thought Yanda would want him to be the one to come to her. He remembered Yanda well, from when she'd come on his boat during the Withum Festival. Somehow, he'd angered her. Of course. Didn't he always? He knew why but couldn't help himself. He'd tried to enter her mind, curious, and she'd blocked him. So, he tumbled her into the ocean. Maybe thought he'd break open her thoughts in surprise. But he hadn't succeeded, had only managed to anger his cousin, Tenali and even Zamani, leader of the Neyna.

He reached for his book, set it back down, threw off his covers, then forced himself to relax against his pillows.

Now that he thought about it, Tenali was the one who'd suggested Yanda go by boat to the festival, probably part of his endless effort to mend the divide between the Elves.

### Yanda

Yanda paced the cramped room. So the Neyla knew she was there. Why did they think she came? They may have seen Tlalit's ship drop her. What would they think of that? She couldn't leave on her own so it may as well be a locked cell. She'd have no idea how to escape. Surely, she'd become lost in those caves and starve. She could mind-call for help. But who? Might they perceive her as a threat to their Power Stone, Ash-Don? Malu had scowled when she asked if the stone was nearby.

Yanda found the catch to open the small bathroom chamber. Intriguing shell devices sprayed warm water.

She showered away the salty sea and dried with a surprisingly soft sea sponge towel.

Back in the sleeping cave, she found a tray of food set on the bed and a sleep gown. She nibbled a few bites of seaweed biscuit and mushroom cheese, then climbed into bed. She expected the sheets to be clammy in this underwater cavern, but they weren't. They were dry.

Her half-elf son could have made the globes dim; he could create light out of nothing. She'd never learned those skills. She missed him with a terrible ache.

Soon she became acutely aware of water and rock surrounding her. How deep under the sea were they? Breathe, she told herself. Curious, she searched the walls and found vents above high shelves. Looking with her sight, she saw they traveled to where land emerged from the sea in rock prominences. What if they got blocked? Would she be smothered?

Feeling alone, she pushed her mind across space to seek her son. But she stopped herself, worried about giving away the rebels' location by anyone who could detect her mind. On the Sarsefi, she'd called him every day on encrypted channels. Instead, she sent feelers for any sentient life within close range. And found a familiar mental register that took her utterly by surprise.

**Mnenu**

After staring at the same plaz page for minutes, Mnenu gave up on reading. At times, he played, sneaking up to hear others' thoughts, even sea creatures, without them detecting him. He sent his mental feelers out toward the Bloob—guest quarters. Training with Ash-don, he had formidable reach now, even without the Circle. He found

Yanda's energy easily, but stopped himself before touching her with his mind. Slowly, patiently, he got closer. And felt her reaching out. Who was she reaching for? He felt her gasp as she found someone but their connection became hidden.

He turned out the light but lay awake, wondering.

## Yanda

"Vatu?" Yanda asked, tentative.

This was insane. Vatu was on Mingal, a planet as far away as you could get in the known universe.

"Yanda?" responded her sweet Mingalian friend—pale blue skin, blue-green head nubs between wisps of white hair, like cornsilk.

"You're not on Mingal?" Yanda asked.

"No, I'm on Terlond. With the Neyla." Vatu conveyed amazement at their connection. "Where are you? You seem close."

"I'm on Terlond, too. Also with the Neyla. Sort of."

"I didn't think you'd return to Terlond, sister."

Yanda's throat tightened with the utterly unexpected presence of her closest friend among the imprisoned talents of Dondar. "Can you tell where I am?" Yanda whispered, barely able to contain her joy. "Do you think you could find me?"

"Yes. I think so. I'm in guest quarters adapted to part amphibious creatures like me. They have such a good set-up for visiting scholars."

"I had no idea. How did you end up here, Vatu?" Yanda asked.

"There are delegations from other planets, all different species. Some from Mingal. You know, we're both water-worlds so we have a lot of science to share. My friend contacted me and as I had no way home yet..."

"Can you come to me?" Yanda was sitting up in bed now, imagining their reunion, fingers toying anxiously, excitedly, with the covers.

"I can. You're not too tired?"

## Mnenu

The sea elf felt Yanda's mental feelers reach out through the stones of the mountain where he'd lived hundreds of years. How could he not sense this new strong mind caressing the walls he knew so well? He detected the vibrations that searched for life, and when she found a mind she knew well, he was surprised. What was their connection? Sleep fled from him.

## Yanda

The thought that her old roommate might join her in this lonely, underwater, membrane-sealed cave-room made Yanda's heart soar. "I'm not too tired. To see you? Never. Please come. Please, please."

"Alright." Vatu laughed. "I'm detecting your location. I'll set off now."

Yanda grinned as she scooted back to the wall and hugged her knees, waiting. There was little else to do.

A quarter of an hour later, Vatu's slight form pushed through the translucent barrier, carrying a bulging bag over her shoulder.

Yanda leapt up and hugged her.

"Tell me everything," Vatu said, dropping her sack. "No, wait." She went out a different wall membrane.

Yanda almost grabbed her to hold her there, hating to lose her from sight so soon.

Vatu pushed back in lugging a folding frame. She left again and returned with bedding. As they went about setting up a second sleeping place, Vatu said, "Tomorrow I'll show you my chamber." She sat on the bed, shoving pillows behind her.

"Like old times," Yanda said, on the bed next to her, choking up again.

"Without Krid and his spy mages watching us." Vatu curled toward her, snuggling into her nest of pillows.

"With freedom to stay or leave," Yanda said.

Vatu pulled her bag up onto the bed and drew out cheeses, mushroom dishes, seaweed flatbreads, and the like.

Yanda added what Malu had brought and they nibbled.

"Now. What's been happening?" Vatu asked.

"You tell first," Yanda said, unready to share about the devastating discovery of her daughter's disappearance and now news that she may have been sighted where Blaz traders were lurking. She just wanted to drink in the sight of her delicate, shape-shifting friend and learn all about her past half a year. Vatu looked so healthy compared to when they'd escaped, even after they'd had weeks in the Elven forest, swimming in natural springs.

"I'll fill you in about me, but I'm bursting to know about you. Where's Zami?"

Yanda's eyes welled with tears. "He's fine. Just let me hear your story first."

## Mnenu

Mnenu detected Vatu in Yanda's room; they'd reduced

their shielding and their thoughts were easy to follow. *Get a grip*, he told himself. *You can ask her about her life. You don't have to eavesdrop.* What was it, this craving to know before he saw her? And he would see her, soon. She wanted the help of the Circle of Ash-don. The more he knew, the better control he felt he'd have. It also seemed like his responsibility, to understand her plight. Lulled by their happy friendship, he let the feelings come, without the words. He finally slept.

## Yanda

"Tell me everything that happened after I left."

Vatu gazed at her, eyes wide with concern. She'd loved Zami from before he was born, had nurtured and cared for him as a second mother his first months. "Fine," she huffed.

"How'd you even get here?" Yanda asked, before Vatu even started.

Vatu laughed. "I actually shifted to a seabird. It was touch and go when other birds came along. I wasn't sure how to act." Vatu put one blue hand over her mouth and snickered to herself. "I had to sit on the surface of the water a lot. I wasn't used to the wing musculature."

"I would have thought you'd swim." Yanda stared, enthralled.

"I wanted a bird's eye view. Do you remember Wondu?" Vatu asked.

"She sat in the Neyla Circle?"

"Exactly. She felt me as I came to rest on the boats out in the atoll. And shifted into a *tesu*. Of course, she could have swum to me as sea elf but she said the *tesu* are so glidy and quick, and strong. I transformed to *tesu* as well. And I've been here since.

"That's kind of how I got here. Have you tried to get home to Mingal?" Yanda asked, uncertain if she could believe the Mingal was truly happy, or just hadn't found a ride.

"I haven't been trying that hard, to tell you the truth." Vatu grinned. "I love it here. They've let me add to the small inter-stellar library. Being in ways similar to my world, and with so many visiting scholars here interested in the same things..." She shrugged. "Now you."

"Well...when I got back to Alland—" Yanda had to wait some seconds to get her voice to work. "Seiti wasn't with my parents."

"Why didn't you tell me?" Vatu asked.

"I've just been so desperate. I went into hiding with some rebels because I was told they were the last who tried to help Seiti find me." She recounted the hours spent, discovering an underground refuge for talents in her home town, finding her apartment taken over by techie nomads, and finally, the exile encampments in Outer Alland. "I was about to settle in and wait for Seiti's return when Tlalit and Merne came to our camp and told me about the sighting on camera."

"And Zami's been living with you in these camps."

"He has a lovely time with Andle's animals." She might have been a tad defensive.

"But what about your ENAC? Didn't you say it's incredibly powerful?"

"I've tried and tried. While still in Skarth, I found a new skill, with AI. It's like it taught me. And I can use it, shielded, to search. I know when I'm shielded. Unlike with people, a logic system can't have hidden motivations. Or it could but I understand how to know... hard to explain. Anyway, I've found other systems. I keep going further and further. It's ... amazing."

Vatu's eyes widened. "Are you sure it's safe, Yanda?"

"Oh, what's safe anymore, Vatu? What am I hiding from? If I can't find my daughter ..."

"I am sorry." Vatu's eyes—with nictating lids—filmed over with tears.

"The last person I spoke to who actually spent time with Seiti, back in Balyou, was the elder, Cillen. She said my daughter was so...mature for her age. I did that to her, Vatu. I made her grow up too fast." Yanda's teeth clenched with self-loathing. She dropped her head to her knees, eyes pressed to her hands, and sobbed the tears she hadn't been able to let loose all these months.

Vatu laid a hand on her shoulder. "Don't blame the victim, Yanda. You were abducted, like all of us. And you helped us escape. You helped the whole planet. The Elves. Maybe the universe. Who knows? If Krid had taken Shalt, once the Stone was whole..." She shrugged her delicate shoulders. "Dondar is getting cleaner and healthier, I hear. Because of you."

"Not just me," Yanda mumbled into her knees. She brought her tear-streaked face up and said, teeth gritted. "Thanks, my friend, but it's not enough. I should have found a way to escape sooner. Should have sent news, communicated. I should have gotten Shouma's help to contact Seiti, tell her so she wouldn't go searching, risk getting picked up by slavers." Her eyes stung.

"She'd already left by the time you could have contacted her. And Krid threatened to hurt your family," Vatu reminded her. "You were keeping them safe."

"Was I? Now Seiti might be trafficked. And they've let Krid free on Farn, to wreak havoc. Why? Why is he free?"

Yanda couldn't hold back her bitterness.

"They're monitoring him, trying to track down the bigger ring of power-collectors. He's connected with Blaz, you know."

Yanda's stomach jerked at this. Did she have the emotional bandwidth to add this to her inner torments? No. Maybe tomorrow. "So, I had Tlalit and Merne drop me in the ocean here."

Vatu grasped Yanda's wrist. "You're so brave. Your world doesn't even have oceans!"

She studied Yanda a moment. "But, they didn't take you home to Rotoul?"

"I insisted they bring me here."

"There's something else, isn't there? What?"

Yanda was silent a moment. "I feel like Zamani wants Zami. I'm not ready to settle with the Neyna. And I can't as long as I'm chasing after Seiti. I won't give up my son."

"How did Merne and Tlalit find you? I thought you were with a hidden underground."

"You know those two. Master networkers." Yanda stared into the distance, seeing nothing, terror gripping her. "What led Seiti to Shagal? Did she think she found a lead?"

"What about the hospital? Did Seiti or your parents contact them?"

"I don't think so. My parents thought I might have been abducted because of my talents, which my mom hates. Thinks they're the work of the devil. She's part of the Church of Vital Promise." Yanda looked into Vatu's otherworldly eyes. "I don't trust her...not to sell me out. Ilan saved me from another sell out."

"Ilan?"

"He was in my apartment, part of the underground that's usurped my home."

Vatu stared at her. "In your city? What's the name, Skarth?"

"They've taken over my apartment as a safehouse. It's apparently ideal for monitoring." Yanda chuckled without real amusement. "Ilan got me away from the group Jelat was bringing me to. But who knows what he's really about? He's brilliant with technologies. His mind might be like a thousand traps."

"But … you're here now. And we're going to find your daughter." Vatu's brows crept up. "What about Tenali?"

"Gone. He said he'd wait to hear from me." Yanda heaved a sigh.

"Maybe something came up," Vatu offered.

"He could find a way to leave me a message. But I am a little worried. Jelat and Arc said they'd watched the Lark from the time we landed."

"Arc?"

"Gods. So many names. I'm sorry."

"In such a short time!" Vatu chuckled, then sobered. "I think you're very important to a lot of people. And beings. Even Stones."

The effort of traveling there suddenly struck Yanda. She yawned, her eyelids heavy. "Let's sleep. We can talk more tomorrow." She wiggled down into the covers.

Vatu did the same, facing her. "I've missed you so much."

"And I you," Yanda mumbled.

Vatu kissed a fingertip and touched Yanda's nose. "Sleep tight, friend."

# CHAPTER

# 15

**Mnenu**

Upon waking, Mnenu remembered their guest. Yanda.

He got out of bed with more vigor than he had for some time. To his surprise, he found himself checking his reflection, putting some time into what he wore, shoving back his long dark hair and retying it. He shook his head with a rueful grin, shoved back stray locks that rarely stayed in place, and headed out for breakfast.

**Yanda**

Yanda opened her eyes, remembering where she was. No light penetrated the room but she looked through the layers of rock and saw early light raying down into the sea.

Vatu sat in her bed, six glow-globes floating over her, writing. "There you are," she said. "Come on. I want you to meet the delegates newly arrived, and a scientist from Mingal..."

Yanda pushed up, rubbing her eyes. "Okay," she said, groggily. This was nothing like she'd expected, coming to the Neyla. She'd pictured coral reefs, pretty fish, and a very insular society of shapeshifting sea elves crafting things out of shells. She had planned to connect with Ash-don and the Circle, get their help to find Seiti. Never had she imagined Vatu and scientific delegations!

"I only have the clothes I arrived in," Yanda said. "And I think they're probably stiff with salt."

"I'll get you something while you shower." Vatu gathered her few items and pushed through to the tunnel.

Yanda imagined herself trying to squeeze into the child-sized Mingal's clothing, and shook her head. "No way." She entered the bath chamber. "How do they filter it?" she wondered as warm, fresh water streamed over her in the shower.

She found a stack of garments when she came out: a tunic and leggings, soft socks and boots, thermal undergarments.

"Humans are usually cold in sea places," Vatu explained, peeking in as Yanda pulled on the layers. "Unless it's tropical."

"Oh, you are right," Yanda said, hugging the warm clothes happily. Alland, with no oceans, kept a relatively even temperature. Cold sea caves were not in her experience.

"You look *nagal*." Vatu grinned. She'd taught Yanda some Mingal words, like this one for beautiful. "Do you remember the meaning?"

"Good, spiffy?"

"Splendid," Vatu said with a flourish of her arm. "Now

come on. I don't want to miss breakfast. After, everyone will go off in all directions."

They pushed through to the first of the outer chambers.

"Are we going to have to swim?" Yanda asked with a sigh. She'd had enough wet for a while.

"They'll dry quickly," Vatu said, puckering in an amused but sympathetic smile. "And this fabric won't hold the salt as much."

Yanda groaned as, after the third membrane, they stepped into a tunnel flowing with sea water.

"Come on." Vatu dove in with delight.

Yanda followed with less joy.

## Mnenu

Mnenu studied the crowd in the dining hall. It was filled with the din of voices high and low, clicking and rasping, along with dishes clattering. There was extra excitement regarding the newcomers. He scanned the two long tables spanning the spacious hall. Where was she? He was about to reach for her with his mind when Talla, his friend since childhood, clapped his shoulder. "Don't take all the *rari*."

Mnenu knocked him with his shoulder. "I think there will be sufficient sustenance for all." With another glance around the hall, he followed Talla to the end of the closer table.

## Yanda

At the far side of the channel, they followed a short labyrinth of hallways, ascending to a higher, lighter level. Vatu threw open a wide door. Still dripping, Yanda stared at the noisy room with its high ceilings. Light penetrating water rayed in through high windows, cast moving motifs on the walls. She shivered, seemingly the only one there who could not dispel wetness. Vatu appeared to absorb moisture the instant she emerged from water.

Malu spotted her from the food line and hurried over. Running her hands along Yanda's arms, she wicked the damp from Yanda's clothes and hair.

Vatu watched. "I have to learn to do that for you."

## Mnenu

Mnenu saw Talla's gaze move toward the doorway, following Malu's figure hurrying in that direction. And spotted the woman who'd cried so powerfully from another planet. He could not have mistaken her.

Had she appeared so striking on his boat? No, this woman was changed: electric, magnificent. Hair just dried by Malu, it stood out in a wild mane, streaks of dark red, near-black in places, highlighted in gold. He sat transfixed.

## Yanda

Yanda took in the two long tables, chatter and clatter filling the air, and gaped at the busy sight. Along the tables were not just tall sea elves but an impressive variety of sentient, partly humanoid creatures.

## Mnenu

Out of the corner of his eye, Mnenu observed as Vatu led Yanda to the food line with its cold and hot dishes, and pick up trays, plates, and utensils. He wondered what Yanda would think of Zotoul's cuisine, after staying with his forest cousins, the Neyna elves. He watched with approval as Yanda took a little of everything. That was open-minded of her, he thought.

## Yanda

The variety of the buffet astounded Yanda, none of it familiar except soft fluffy buns that resembled ones served in the Elven forest, dotted with mushrooms, olives, or fruits.

Vatu led the way to empty seats at a table lively with conversation.

Yanda sat and bit into smoked fish. "Mmm…" She tried a dark paste and made a face. "Glad I didn't take too much of that." She delicately pushed it to one side.

Vatu giggled. "Rari eggs. I haven't quite acquired a taste for them either."

"What's a *rari*?" Yanda asked. She felt eyes on her—with a disturbing energy that was oddly familiar. Looking around, she found the source at the head of the other table. After all this time, the heat of anger rose up her neck to her cheeks. She glared at Mnenu and turned purposefully away. To distract herself, she spoke to a sea-being across from her. "I'm Yanda."

"I am called Takmik," a walrus-like humanoid answered, intonations vibrating. He bowed slightly, as his nasal cavities and mouth pursed in and out like sphincters.

"Takmik." Yanda did her best to pronounce the name which clicked in a way unfamiliar to her and hoped she approximated the sounds. "Nice to meet you."

Her mind coursed back to Mnenu. He was beautiful, the most captivating Elf she'd seen. Yet he'd been arrogant and hadn't appealed to her in the least. He seemed to assume she'd find him attractive and be under his spell. His smile was more a leer, she thought.

## Mnenu

Mnenu sensed her turn toward him. He was sure she recognized him but her look was not friendly. In fact, she appeared to hate him. She turned away, frowning.

He thought back to that day almost a year ago when he'd hosted her on his boat. What had gone wrong? Well, he'd thrown her in the sea. Why couldn't he have controlled himself? And how would she respond when she found out she had to come to him if she wanted to sit in the Circle and speak to Ash-don? She might leave instead. He didn't want her to. He didn't want that at all.

## Yanda

Yanda noticed Vatu's hand on her arm.

"This is Alyena. From my planet." Vatu leaned back to introduce the Mingal fem next to her.

Alyena was slightly larger than Vatu, her skin tone a warm green with hints of orange around her eyes and lips, her head nubs a rich rust brown, but she shared Vatu's delicate frame.

"I'm happy to meet you, Alyena," Yanda said.

"Likewise." Alyena gave her a bright smile.

They continued eating companionably.

Yanda asked Alyena, "Did you just arrive from Mingal?"

Vatu shook her head. "She was already studying on Erlot." She paused to take a bite and chew. "So was I..."

Yanda stared at her. "When Krid captured you?"

She again felt Mnenu's eyes on her. He had a way of forcing his presence.

## Mnenu

Mnenu couldn't help watching, and trying to read their conversation though Yanda was half-turned away. He lightly touched her mind, hoping to catch thoughts. Anything.

Talla said, "You keep staring over there. Is it the Xentu witch who fascinates you?"

"Why do you call her that?" Mnenu drawled, feigning casual interest as he bit into rari on toast.

"Well, you know what they say. And that shout—"

"Yes, I know she's of the Xentu, most likely. I'm just saying where'd you get the witch part? Because she has powers?" He was sounding proprietary. He'd better tone it down.

"Sure. She has weird skills. How do we know she can't blast as well as pull a great stone together? I mean, she has a temper, clearly."

"Why do you say that?" Mnenu shoveled in another bite, trying to keep calm.

"The shout. Everyone heard it."

"How do you even know what it was about?" Mnenu snapped at his oldest friend.

"I don't." Talla shoved off Mnenu's shoulder as he got up. "Coming to the reefs?"

"Can't today."

"Oh, yeah. You're the Voice." Talla gave him a crooked grin but there was something else in his eyes.

# A FAR CRY

## Yanda

Why had he angered her so much? All he'd done was jump off the rigging, taking her with him into the sea where they swam with the *tesu*. But he had been storming her with his thoughts before that. It wasn't right. It was shocking, like…like an assault.

Maybe it had felt too much like Krid. Kridenit, who'd put her in a trance with his mind, then violated her and held her hostage all the time she was pregnant. He'd kept mage spies on her and the other nine fems he's collected—his captives, his treasures, each with mind-powers. It had taken them over a year to finally escape the compound and reach the Elven forest.

Was Mnenu really as bad as she'd made him out to be, though? He was Tenali's friend, after all. Cousin, even. Tenali'd explained that he was just overly enthusiastic. But that had been dismissive. Mansplaining. He obviously knew him differently.

Yanda brought her mind back to Vatu who'd said something more to her. Diners were beginning to get up, put plates on rolling carts, and move toward the doors, in animated conversation, or alone. "I'm sorry. You were saying…you were both in school on Erlot."

Vatu laughed. "Your thoughts were a million miles away. What were you thinking of? You scowled for a second." She followed Yanda's gaze to the male Neyla speaking to someone near him, eyes occasionally darting toward Yanda. "Is that Mnenu? Didn't you go on his boat?" Vatu searched Yanda's face.

"I did."

"I thought you had fun." There was a question in Vatu's voice.

"It was fun. I just…"

Was he listening? It was as though she felt his mind pressing. Did she imagine it? Yanda dropped her voice low. "Do you feel his mind? It's always…loud to me." Yanda shifted uncomfortably in her seat. "Pushy."

"Uh… I haven't noticed. Maybe it's aimed just to you." Vatu spoke quietly. "Do you want to come with us to the library? We don't go through water to get there." She grinned. "And I can show you my rooms."

Yanda nodded, smiling with relief. "I'd love to see both." He still looked at her. Was there a smirk on his face now?

# CHAPTER

# 16

**Mnenu**

Mnenu saw Vatu glance in his direction. Now he watched as they got up. Where would they go? Would she leave the planet without ever seeking the Circle's help? Because of him? He smiled, derisive. How could he turn this around?

As she got up to leave with the Mingals, he stood as well.

**Yanda**

Oh, no, she groaned inside. He's getting up, too. But he did not approach. He only gave a slight bow in her direction.

Vatu grabbed her sleeve. Yanda turned toward Takmik, wishing she knew a polite way to leave this dignified creature. She gave a little wave. He leaned in a semi-bow, eyes blinking sideways.

They joined others placing dishes in bins by the wall, and started toward a set of doors at the far end. Yanda noticed Mnenu watching them, then leave through a side door with a Neyla of similar height and weight to his—tall, broad shouldered, pale green-brown skin, hair braided thickly over the top, and hanging past his shoulders, small sea objects woven in.

Yanda hadn't realized she'd stopped to watch them.

Vatu again studied her. "What is it?" Vatu asked again. "Did he do something to you?"

"I'm sorry. No. Not really. It was just—"

Malu called out, running to them, "Can I join you? I'd love to see what you're doing in the library."

Yanda had to wonder, was Malu assigned to keep an eye on her? How did she even know they were going to the library?

"Of course," Vatu said, hooking arms with Malu and Yanda. "Alyena has done so much more than I have."

Alyena linked Yanda's other arm.

Frescoes of sky scenes covered the high walls and ceilings as though to comfort those unused to living underwater.

Yanda gazed up and around her, happy to be in this companionable group, and not in Mnenu's presence. That is, until she remembered her errand here and her mood darkened. She was slowly going mad, having no contact with her daughter. Now she missed her little boy with a deep ache as well. She'd been away two and a half weeks. Soon—maybe tomorrow—she'd ask if they could use the encrypted lines to call Andle as she'd done from the Sarsefi.

At the end of the beautiful hallway, Vatu threw open

wide doors to reveal a lavish room filled with books on shelves, with balustrades winding around, rising from the central foyer to levels above. The top was a dome that allowed light in. Yanda suspected at higher tide it slipped underwater and darkened. "Wow." She stared upward, feet glued to the tile flooring.

"Want to see the Alland section?" Vatu asked, at her elbow.

"I want to see your rooms," Yanda said.

Vatu appeared surprised but acquiesced. They left the other two talking over a display.

"You spoke constantly about the lack of books when we were captive," Vatu said, as they climbed a curving stairway. "I thought you'd want to spend more time in the library."

**Mnenu**

Mnenu and Valla walked along a corridor splashed by sea-waves.

"Where were they going?" his friend asked.

"I imagine the library." Mnenu wished he could have gone with them.

"How about those Mingals?"

"What about them?" Mnenu fought the urge to leap off the side into the sea. He had things to do, though.

"I've heard they can transform into anything." Valla leaned down to pick up a shell and blow its end.

"We transform." Mnenu wondered what Valla was meaning. He was catching thoughts about their head-nubs.

"Mostly into sea creatures," Valla countered.

"I wonder if some of the Neyna have worked more on

those skills. I heard Merne can be anything."

They entered the inside halls that led to Mnenu's office and he was glad Valla didn't elaborate on what seemed like a rude thought.

## Yanda

"I do love books. I just want to see where you've been living." Yanda wasn't sure what the real reason was. Maybe she wanted to test if Malu would let her out of sight.

She was also dreading returning to her little hole alone. She wondered if there was something about the others' rooms she couldn't survive.

They navigated a complex of hallways, some splashed with waves, seeming to head upward, until they stepped over a reef-like sill in a doorway lined in coral. Vatu's chamber resembled a refined cave, mottled with alcoves, high areas reached by curving steps. Windows angled to fit the walls. Some were sealed tightly and let in pale sea-colored light. The lower areas could get wet. Yanda remember Vatu's stories of her own world, Mingal, where they lived half-in, half-out of sea caverns and never minded the water. Their clothing and furnishings were made to withstand, even invite, moist environments. Vatu's skin had a delicate rubber texture and her body temperature acclimatized to her surroundings.

"May I?" Yanda took a step onto a narrow stairway that climbed to a curved door.

"Yes. Come. See it all." At the top of the steps, Vatu parted a tightly overlapping seal and slid through.

This room was an eyrie looking out to sea.

"This driest one is for electronics and books. My office, I guess." Vatu waved the globe lights up to full luminosity.

There were books, plaz docs, a wide couch with pillows and quilts, and a warming globe set into the base of the far wall. On a tiny, ornate shelf, Yanda spotted the collection of shells and stones Vatu had with her in Dondar, and a photo of Yanda and Zami. She walked over and picked it up. "When was this taken?"

"Tlalit gave it to me."

"You've stayed in touch?" Yanda's heart beat with nervous thuds. "Wait, this is in their underground tech lair, in Rotoul, isn't it? I recognize the subterranean gardens." She felt relief that it wasn't taken of them on Alland. Tlalit could have, she had not doubt, tracked down images anywhere she went. Still, it would seem invasive. "She gave it to you? Here?"

"As far as I know, they've never been here." Vatu joined her and studied the pic. "They sent it. I plazzed it. Do you have recent ones of our Zami-boy?"

"I do. Lots. But I didn't bring a device."

"Want to sign onto my Lalut?" Vatu stepped to her desk, sat and tapped a prism-shaped computer awake.

Vatu and Yanda had never been on electronics together; no device had been allowed during their captivity on Terlond. Well, once in the Elven forest, Yanda had been on computer, in the advanced catacomb of screens and hard-drives dominated by Merne and Tlalit. It was strange to contemplate, but every bit of this time with Vatu was unexpected.

Vatu brought the hand-held to the couch and they huddled together, shoulder-to-shoulder, as Yanda found images of Zami, running after NikNik, the rescued marsupial baby; on Andle's porch trying to help sift flour for baking; in a bath made of a barrel heated over ambient fire; riding in a pack on Setoin's back.

Vatu brought the device close and expanded the photo to show Zami's laughing face.

Yanda swallowed a knot. "I'd like to call him. We connected, encrypted, from Tlalit's ship."

"You've been on the *Sarsefi*. Wow." Vatu sounded envious.

They grinned over the ship's name, meaning "love-making" in Neyna.

"Tlalit says it makes love to the stars, or tries to." She laughed, gazing at her son's face on the screen. "She told me as she and Merne gave moony eyes at each other."

"I can imagine." Vatu wiggled sideways on the couch. "You didn't watch them through the walls, did you?"

Yanda primly assured her she didn't.

"Mm-hm." Vatu smirked.

"Didn't." Yanda shoved her shoulder and their laughter felt incredibly good. It'd been a long time.

Someone tapped on the door. "Can I join?" Alyena called.

"Of course. Come," Vatu invited.

## Mnenu

In his lavish office, previously held by his mother, Mnenu sent the lightest touch across the sea mountain city to the Mingal's quarters. Most visiting scholars who could live partially in the sea were housed in that northern area.

As when he wanted to observe sea life in a distant cave, he let his awareness settle gently through the walls. He all but "saw" Yanda and the two Mingals crowded onto the couch, laughing and chatting. He enjoyed the sight.

## Yanda

Yanda scooted down the couch for the other Mingal to settle in by Vatu and the three fell into conversation. Yanda and Vatu talked about their time of captivity and escape, Yanda about the rebel camp, Vatu and Alyena about their school times.

"You were gone all night," Alyena said to Vatu.

"I stayed with Yanda in the Bloober," Vatu responded.

"Thank the gods she did," Yanda said. "I was feeling a little suicidal, surrounded by rock and sea and…nobody I knew of nearby." Yanda sank down into the corner, remembering her first hour. "Alyena, do you have your own rooms?"

"Yes, close," Alyena said. "I can show you."

"They give you both very honored accommodations, it seems like," Yanda commented.

"They do. We've been very well treated."

"Well, your world is like this, mostly sea. It's easier to set you up. And it must be valuable for them, to have scientists like you visit and contribute to their library." Yanda put this together as she spoke, hating the thought of returning to her isolated guest chamber.

## Mnenu

Picking up her thought, Mnenu sat up. He should plan for better quarters for her. He could quickly have a room adapted for her, one as nice as Vatu's or better. He was about to call his engineers when he heard Vatu say, "You won't go back to the Bloober. You'll stay with me."

He watched as the three left the room, chattering about

fetching Yanda's belongings from the far away module.

"Did you leave Malu in the library?" Yanda asked Alyena as they walked.

"No. She had to go to a meeting."

He wondered why Yanda asked. Then caught the thread of her thoughts. She suspected Malu had been assigned to watch her. Why would she think that? He heard her thought, *At least the Mingals aren't in on monitoring my movements.*

*Why did she think they would spy on her?* he wondered.

He watched them return, stopping to grab snacks from a to-go buffet set out in the cafeteria at midday. Vatu made the couch in her office into a bed for Yanda, piling thick quilts and pillows on it, snugged up to a sea wall with a tightly sealed window that would at times be underwater, and hoped she'd be happy.

He needed to pull his head into his duties.

## Yanda

The bed with fluffy quilts called to Yanda and she yawned massively.

"I think we need to let you nap," Vatu said.

It was true; though she'd been terribly glad to find Vatu in that strange sea-city, and to have her company, she had not slept all that well.

Vatu brought her a nightgown and Yanda climbed in under the covers. Vatu kissed her cheek and left.

Glad for privacy, Yanda also felt sad hearing the two Mingals chattering in their own tongue, laughing softly.

After a while they called "Good night"

It's only afternoon, she mumbled.

Did she feel a pang of jealousy not to have Vatu to

herself, as she had, so much of the time, for a year and a half? They'd always positioned their beds side by side. She'd listened for the Mingal's breathing, helped clear her congestion. And Vatu had watched out for her, transformed her when she needed to hide, helped care for Zami.

Though she luxuriated in the soft bedding, she slept fitfully. The tide rose and the room darkened. Was it day or night? In the middle of what she thought was night, she woke terrified.

# CHAPTER

# 17

## Mnenu

**M**nenu found himself suddenly awake. Yanda was troubled. He'd felt it.

Why was he so connected to her? Well, he'd been tapping in on her thoughts and set a conduit, a path between them, it seemed. Now he caught her thoughts without seeking them. Why did she think her daughter might be imprisoned by the Blaz? He sat up and formed a glow-globe with his mind to light the room. Had she dreamed that? He followed her terrified thoughts deeper, finding memories. No, Tlalit and Merne had shown her a video of a girl her daughter's age, in Blenin, just before a Blaz ship left the moon.

No wonder she was desperate enough to be dumped in their seas, not even knowing how to swim, to get answers. To get their help.

That's when her mind had bellowed that cry, heard

across the universe. He scowled at Talla's careless remark about a temper. Xentu witch, he'd called her, knowing nothing about her troubles.

## Yanda

Lying still in her covers on the couch, Yanda heard water sloshing against the window next to her and felt suddenly buried underwater. Sometimes it seemed like she was adjusting to life in the undersea city; other times, it felt smothering. She brought the sheet to her face, bunched, wringing it, until she managed to re-enter sleep.

## Mnenu

Feeling Yanda settle, he again curled under his own covers and put out the light.

She seemed troubled by the water rising to surround her room. Maybe he could make a place more comfortable for her after all.

## Yanda

Yanda woke. Getting on her knees, she peered out the oval window near her at a calm sea touched by the rose-orange tones of this world's sun. The last of the three moons remained in the morning sky, an opalescent-blue crescent, hovering near the edge of the world.

Vatu popped her head in, seeming to have heard her wake. "Get up, sleepy. We don't want to miss breakfast."

"You go along. I want to stare at this view. There's no ocean on my world, you know." With the light, all Yanda's nightmarish thoughts vanished, and she sat, caped in covers, staring out at sea birds whirling.

"I do know. I'll bring you something." Vatu turned to leave.

"I want to speak with the Circle today." Yanda's most pressing mission was for Ash-don to help her find her daughter. "And also, I'd like to call home, to talk to Zami. Do you know who could help me?"

She turned away from the view.

## Mnenu

Mnenu slept a bit late after his disrupted slumber in the dead of night. Scrambling to wash and dress, he hurried to breakfast. He'd be expected to greet the new visitors, some from Langry. Their worlds had a new agreement; Langrians had never before come to them. Reaching the hall, where many had already gotten their food, he scanned the faces for Yanda. She wasn't there yet.

Disappointed, he loaded his plate. His parents signaled for him to sit with them. Filling a cup with *krenla*, he joined them.

## Yanda

Yanda saw Vatu's eyes drop to her lap and realized she was wringing her hands.

"Did you get enough sleep?" Vatu asked, studying her face.

"I think I had a nightmare," Yanda remembered. "I'm so worried about my daughter, it's hard to think about anything else."

"More reason for you to come to the hall with us," Vatu pushed.

"I'd rather not." Yanda looked down at the night-gown Vatu had loaned her—webby and too short, but very soft. Her own clothes were more suited for Alland's outback.

"Are you worried about clothes? We can loan you some. We didn't get dropped into the ocean here." She paused. "Well, Alyena brought me some. And they shipped my belongings from the university at Erlot."

## Mnenu

Mnenu ate, listening to his parents and several other elders around the table debate issues of supplies. He tested the temperature of his *krenla*. Finding it hot, he set it aside and spread sweet jelly on a roll. Chewing, his mind drifted to Yanda, just as Vatu asked her about clothing. It seemed she was refusing to come to breakfast.

She needed clothes! Of course. She'd landed in their ocean with nothing. But what had she worn yesterday? It had been quite attractive. Maybe borrowed. She should be told where to acquire clothing.

He realized his mother was glaring at him and, with reluctance, attuned to the conversation.

## Yanda

"I'm so glad they shipped you your things," Yanda said. "That you've been in touch with your family. They must have been relieved to hear from you. And anxious to see you."

Vatu frowned. "There's something else. Is it…Mnenu? Can't you tell me why he bothers you?"

Yanda rubbed her eyes. "I don't know. He threw me into the sea. He was just playing, Tenali assured me. But he did a weirdly powerful mind-drilling before that. Then he jumped down and took me into the water with him. I'd never even been in deep water."

"That sounds awful." Vatu sat at the end of her bed and squeezed her foot.

"Out of the blue, I'm hit like a thunderbolt, and we're flying through the air, and plunging deep into the sea." Yanda toyed with a tassel on a pillow. "He didn't even ask." Her voice trailed off. "But it's a long time ago now."

"You told Tenali and he just sluffed it off?"

"Yeah." Yanda shrugged. "I know they're friends."

"Or cousins. Don't ask me the lineage." Vatu took Yanda's hand and stroked it, looking up at her with concerned eyes.

It was hard to re-create it in a way that didn't seem like kids frolicking in the water.

"I understand." Vatu looked earnest. "And now? Did you get a bad feeling from him yesterday?"

"Just intense. I don't know why he kept staring at me."

"You won't let him keep you from eating, will you? You can sit between me and Alyena. Face away from him. I think you'd have more chance of setting up a session with the Circle. We'll have to find out how you might call Zami."

"Okay." Yanda threw off the blankets. "You make a good point."

**Mnenu**

Again letting his mind drift, this time from the topic of

reef-protection and overuse, Mnenu heard Yanda agree to come to the dining hall. His heart sped up.

He could see the others from her mind, though could not get into the Mingal minds as easily. *Why was that*?

Through Yanda's eyes, he saw Alyena peek in. "Want to wear this?" She held up an outfit, shades of green and gold, like velvet, with shells worked in along elaborate brocade edges. She was a bit taller than Vatu. It looked like it might come to Yanda's mid-calf. The Mingal scholar also held out leggings and the malleable boots of Zotoul. "I think they'll fit."

He agreed and looked forward to seeing her wearing them.

"That's so kind of you." Yanda climbed out of bed.

He caught an image of the far-too-small, nubbly nightgown she'd borrowed, most likely from Vatu, and grinned.

"Mnenu." His father's peremptory bark brought him back to the dining table.

"Sorry."

"This will be your job soon enough," his father reprimanded. "You won't always just play with sitting in the Circle, mind-melding with Ash-don, swimming and boating. What a life you lead."

### Yanda

"They look awfully fancy, though." Yanda eyed the clothes.

"No, just normal wear when you're visiting scholars." Alyena grinned. Her incisors were pointier than Vatu's. She brought the outfit over.

"Wash up quick," Vatu said. "I want these on you."

Already clothed—Vatu in browns and deep greens, Alyena in autumn orange with rust highlights—they appeared to be wearing beautiful coral reefs.

During captivity, Yanda had only seen Vatu in one outfit from her home planet that grew shabby over the year and a half, after constant wear. The Terlondian servants had taken pity and given them mismatched, discarded outfits of dubious design. Yanda had never known how Vatu dressed on Mingal but had imagined diving suits for navigating the sea world they occupied. Not these lovely ensembles.

The bath chamber was much more elaborate than the guest one she'd first used. This one was beautifully tiled and spacious. Quickly, she showered, toweled off, and put on Alyena's clothes. They fit adequately, though snugger than she would normally wear.

The three left for the dining hall. Before they'd even entered, Yanda heard a roar of activity. At the doorway, she stopped to scan the busy diners.

## Mnenu

At last, Mnenu saw Yanda's figure in the doorway. Her hair was clipped up, the contrasting shades of dark red, black and gold, if anything, more entrancing, enhanced by the gold-green clothing. Many around the hall turned to look at her; conversation dropped a few decibels.

He longed to jump up and hurry to her, show her the best of the dishes served that morning, check in about her nightmare.

It was wrong of him to know what she was thinking. He should be patient and wait for her to tell him what was on her mind. But would she?

At least she had not left the planet.

**Yanda**

Pulled toward the food by her Mingal companions, Yanda looked over the many tall Neyla with their swirling eyes and pointed ears. Most were slender, Mnenu slightly brawnier than the average—which might help her pick him out from the crowd.

Malu spotted them and waved, signaling for them to join her. They acknowledged and lined up for plates, examining the choices on the long side tables: new types of brightly colored fish eggs, fried and scrambled *sala* eggs garnished with toasted seaweed and *tika* seeds, sweet biscuits, bright crimson *aspar* juice, and of course, *kran* or *krenla* with crema.

Joining Malu, they greeted those around them at the table. Yanda dipped the tip of her spoon into *weejon* egg paste and tasted. Unlike yesterday's, this one was delicious. She thought about getting more.

Malu said, "I've set up an audience for you with the leader of the Circle. I know you want to ask Ash-don for help." She smiled, looking pleased with herself.

"That's great. When?" First matter of business accomplished, she'd wait before requesting communication with her son.

"When you finish eating." Malu dug into her meal.

That soon. Yanda's heart beat faster.

**Mnenu**

At last, his parents got up and left; after all, they'd arrived a good long while before him.

Watching their proud, slightly sloping shoulders exit the hall, he let his senses drift out to where Yanda sat, further down the table, with her friends.

In her mind, he heard Malu tell her she'd set up a meeting. He and Malu had scheduled it the day before. He felt her excitement and nervousness. How would she have reacted had she known it was him she would be meeting? Playing with his food, he willed her not to hate him.

# Part III

# CHAPTER

# 18

Yanda went back to the serving tables and helped herself to more saffron paste. Anxious for her meeting, she ate quickly. "Did you hear?" she said in a low voice to Vatu. "I have a meeting with the Circle leader after breakfast."

"Fantastic!" Vatu nibbled on a sweet biscuit coated with pale green jam. "Who is it?"

"She didn't say. What's on your sweet roll? I didn't see that."

"It's from the *hajar* fruit. Not far from here are atolls with fruit orchards. Try it." Vatu scooped a small amount onto Yanda's plate.

Yanda spread it on a corner of her roll and tasted. "Yum. Where'd you find it?"

"I'll get you more. I'm going to get a *kran* refill." Vatu got up.

"Thanks." Yanda pushed fish eggs onto her *sala* scramble and tried a bite.

Diners were leaving the tables.

She ruminated on her upcoming conversation. They wouldn't refuse to help her, would they? Well, if they did, she'd have to consider returning to the continent to ask the Neynas' Circle, though she didn't have much hope. She and Shalt had been in close mind-meld for days when she'd helped bring the stone back to wholeness. Surely thoughts of her daughter had touched the Great Stone's awareness. But Shalt had not conveyed any information about her daughter leaving their home planet.

Vatu returned and handed her a tiny dish of the bright green jam.

"Thanks." Yanda kissed Vatu's cheek as she sat. "You're the best. I think I'll just eat a few more bites and then try to get time with the Circle." Now that it was set up, she could think of little else.

Vatu squeezed her hand. "I'm sure it's on your mind."

Yanda gulped down the last of her *kran* and got up to take her dirty dishes to the clean-up cart.

Malu joined her. "Ready?"

"I am." Yanda waved to Vatu who watched her go, eyes anxious.

Some floors below, Yanda and Malu walked side-by-side down an elegant corridor Yanda had never seen, with high vaulted ceilings. They turned inward from colonnaded walks splashed by the sea. Their destination lay deep in the sea-mountain city, down steep carpeted stairs where the only light was from elaborate glow-globes containing underwater scenes with sea creatures.

Through a sealed doorway, they entered a small vestibule lined floor-to-ceiling, with thick sumptuous rugs of somber sea colors: browns, darkest green, with hints of gold. Heavy, carved benches lined the walls.

"I'll leave you here." Malu pointed to a door etched in deep relief.

All this pomp and ceremony, Yanda thought, glancing down at the clothes she wore. Now she was glad Alyena had given her a dressy outfit. They'd even put her wild mane of hair into twists on her head, held with decorative crystal and mother-of-pearl clasps.

Having no idea what or who to expect, she knocked on the elaborate door. Hearing nothing, she turned the polished brass handle and shoved. The heavy door swung open. A Neyla Elf stood with his back to her, hands clasped behind, dark hair in a braid.

She walked forward, the thick carpet muffling her steps. She cleared her throat, readying to speak, to explain her request, heart thundering, when the Elf turned.

She gasped. He must have been hiding his mind energy or she'd have known who it was instantly. "Oh," she said. "You're the…leader of the Circle."

He wore a magnificent, fitted jacket, and satin pants of a dark burgundy, well fitted to his strong thighs that could powerfully pump through deep ocean waters, so powerfully he could shoot above the waters carrying…her.

But this did not seem like the frisky Neyla Elf who'd frolicked in the sea with her, swimming with the *tesu*, laughing, whistling in their language.

Okay, that part had been appealing, but he'd stormed a mental energy at her first, seeming to want to freeze her or something. What had been his intention? When he'd grabbed her, launching with her into the ocean, he'd scared her.

As Mnenu turned fully to face her, she felt a frisson

of that same energy vibrating toward her, but controlled now. He stepped closer, and spoke in a soft low voice. "I didn't know I'd frightened you so much last year."

She started. Had she lost so much of Shouma's teaching that she couldn't shield her thoughts? Did he have a mind-power she couldn't shut out?

Mnenu looked uncomfortable. "Sit." He indicated a thickly brocaded seat that faced his impressive desk of dark polished wood. He sat in a high-backed swiveling chair facing her.

She studied his face. He'd always been handsome, but she'd rejected that thought after he'd become, to her, just a rough lout.

"I apologize," he said again. "Just because I can hear you does not mean I should listen. I could close it out. But I was curious. Your body stance said so much once you recognized me." He sat back and crossed his legs.

Now she saw the more arrogant side returning.

"I admit, your manner yesterday should have given me a clue," he said. "I thought I was being inviting." He laughed at himself.

"Um. A little intense." Yanda didn't want to discourage him from helping her. Now she was in a new position; she felt glad he was contrite, but she needed something from him. She did not like this new dynamic. It made her feel hypocritical, fawning. She ran her fingers along grooves in the chair arms that ended in curled claws.

"Can I get you water? Kran?" he asked.

It was hard to give up her anger. She realized she'd harbored it for a while. And now that she was admitting things to herself, had her need to nurse anger started in a far deeper place? Krid, perhaps? She'd been molested, held captive even through giving birth and the first months of her baby's life. Yet had never been able to express to the foul mage how much she loathed him for it all, even when she was helping to vanquish him and his army.

She raised her eyes. "You startled me, back then, on the boat. It seemed like...your mind communication felt..." How to describe it? Overpowering? "...rough," she settled on. She glanced up as he winced. "I'd never been in an ocean. Never been around them. My world has none."

"I'm sorry." Mnenu folded his hands on the desktop. "I'm afraid I get rather wild when I spend long stretches on the sea. I swim with the *tesu* like my brothers and sisters, and we wrestle and bump each other. It must have been jarring for you."

"I might also have needed a target for pent-up anger," Yanda admitted.

"You'd been through a lot."

Yanda'd never imagined such a conversation with this Elf. "I wondered why your mental energy felt so...forceful." Her hands explored the clawed ends of the chair arms.

Mnenu seemed to ponder, appearing embarrassed. Finally, he said, "This 'big' energy is why I was selected as Ash-don's voice. I think it's not easy for a lot of people to be around. That's why I spent long stretches at sea. I'm more—" he flicked a glance at her— "trained now."

"Oh." Yanda was at a loss for words.

"Not to say I wouldn't take a tumble in the sea with you if given—" He stopped, checking her response, mischief creeping in.

"I hope you might ask first next time," she said, wiggling up straighter in her seat. Fawning be damned. She had her pride.

"Indeed. I hope I would, as well." He set his arms on the desk and leaned toward her. "You seek your daughter." His manner was serious now.

"You know?"

"Tenali told me, yes."

Yanda's heart sped up. She sat forward. "You're in touch with him?" Was he on Terlond? Electricity shot from her heart to her belly and downward.

"No. Not recently. When you came here, I remembered the story."

"Why didn't you ask me? Oh." She remembered how inviting he'd been the day before. "I'm sorry. I wasn't very friendly yesterday."

He flicked a hand, dismissive. "You have great worries," he said, generously, but his mouth quirked. They both knew why she'd avoided him.

She pressed her hands into her lap. "Will you allow me into the Circle with Ash-don?"

"Yes. I must ask, though, why you did not return to Shalt for help. You are so profoundly tied. Why you did not ask for help from the Neyna, who aided in your escape and hosted you? Why—" he folded his hands again on the desk and leaned forward— "did you not bring Zami, Zamani's son, when you were escorted here by his aunt and her *fajan*?"

He certainly had stepped into a leader's role. Yanda raised her hands to stop this flow of recriminations. "Okay! I know. I..." Jeez. She'd really not thought through the storm of controversy her choices would cause. "I'm a thoughtless renegade."

She tried to read his expression, which comprised only of a slight lift of his eyebrows. Thinking about it, she realized, this was true. She hadn't been a rebel before Shalt called her across the universe, causing her to abandon her daughter who was now missing and believed, possibly, to be with the most dangerous and cruel traders of the known universe.

But now she could be considered a rebel.

Mnenu threw himself against the back of his chair and guffawed, startling her. "Ha! Well, I did feel your shout from Alland. Quite a bellow! Talk about *my* mind powers."

"You heard… How could you hear it?"

With pleasure, he announced, "That was Shaltborn." Then he sobered. "Sometimes when we've been the voice of these Stones, we develop an unruly streak."

"Hmm." She knew she'd changed after melding with the Stone's energy, but she'd not put any of this together. Instead of continuing in the same vein, she asked, "Where is Tenali?"

Mnenu's smile lost its delight. "Off looking for your daughter, so I understand. He did always want to be the hero."

"Looking for—" Yanda stared. "Did Merne tell you?" That's where he went? Why had he said nothing? Yanda could have gone with him.

Mnenu stared off into the distance for a moment. "Is there anything else I can help you with, until the Circle is ready for you?"

It struck Yanda with clear force: Mnenu was jealous when she asked passionately about Tenali.

For the first time, she felt, or heard—she couldn't tell which—a rumbling under the chamber that vibrated in her chest. It seemed to be increasing, filling the air.

"Is that Ash-don?"

But she'd been dismissed.

Mnenu stood and walked toward the outer door.

Yanda stood as well. "Just a small thing, I hope. I'd like a connection to where my son is, on Alland. I have the codes for an encrypted channel."

"That's no problem." Mnenu was all business now.

As she approached, he took her and pressed his forehead to hers in the Elven way. She felt a smattering of the powerful energy that had struck her so forcefully on his boat, now tinged with sweet warmth. He let her go and she stumbled back as the energy released her.

He stepped away. "Kalden will take you to a radial matrix."

A side door swung open and a young Neyla—young in terms of demeanor and attire, at least; there was no telling the age of any of the Elves—stepped through. Tats and piercings adorned his face, neck, and arms. He wore a sleeveless vest and pants that clinked with tiny metal objects, like some of the Neyna.

"Come this way." Kalden signaled to her. "I like your outfit. Is it Mingalian?"

"It is, yeah," she said, glancing down at Alyena's elegant clothing, flexible as thin sea kelp, fine as woven moss.

Kalden grinned back at Mnenu as they left, but the lead Neyla—Ash-Don's voice—had already turned away to his book shelves.

# CHAPTER

# 19

S he wondered what Mnenu had thought of her clothes. Why was she wondering that? she berated herself.

They exited through an obscured doorway and Kalden trotted easily up a spiral staircase. Yanda panted behind.

At each floor, intriguing hallways stretched away, lined in doorways, or books, or sea walks with splashing waves. The walls of the final hallway narrowed to a rounded tower. They rose in a lift that took in undersea views, of tall kelp, an eel, silvery fishes in schools, before they stepped into an octagonal tower room. Behind it, they entered a tunnel carved from rough-hewn rock. It was one completely sealed from the sea with the layered membranes stretched at entrances. Skylights let in natural light from the domed roof. Otherwise, the room was lit only by tech screens and glow-globes.

Kalden slid into a tall swivel chair and invited Yanda

to take the one next to him. He pressed his fingers to her temples and she instinctively gave him Andle's encrypted code.

Another male Neyla, long braids hanging at his back, the sides of his head shaven in patterns with tattoos, entered and started to sit at another terminal but Kalden said softly to him in Neyla, *"Arspat tinas kahay, Werhi."*

The other Neyla nodded with a kind smile at Yanda, and left, closing off the hallway that skewered the sea mountain's highest peak.

Once they were alone again, Kalden pointed to a key. "After I'm out, press this. You can wear these." He plugged in headphones. "When you're done, call me here." He indicated a button on the wall.

She nodded. "Thank you." Her pulse hammered in her throat as she pressed the key he'd shown her and waited. The screen in front of her shifted to a spiraling pattern and beeped lightly.

Then her sweet boy's face filled the screen and she let out a cry. "Baby Button." Her eyes filled with tears she batted away.

"Meh-meh," Zami crowed. "Elspie!" He showed her a tiny baby rodent that must have recently been born, wiggling and sniffing in his chubby hand.

Andle's face came into view by his shoulder. "Doing okay?" she asked.

"Good. You?" Yanda responded with a tight throat.

"Champion." Andle kissed Zami's cheek. "Aren't we?"

"Zami help An-dan."

"He sure does," Andle agreed, ruffling his curls. "We have to move soon. I'll give you coordinates the instant I know."

"Oh, fudge. You have to? I'm expecting to be done

soon here." Yanda had hoped to be back before any rebel camp movement. Being away from her son made her powerless enough without further danger indicated by their need to change location.

She sent an extra cone of protection around her so that no words could be discerned outside her bubble. "I've gained an audience with the Power Stone of the Neyla. I'm not sure when, but as soon as I know where my daughter is, I'll be back to you and Zami."

"You're doing okay?" Andle asked. "What's it like? You live in the ocean?"

Yanda had told her of the city under the sea she'd seen with Tenali. "Parts of the city are built into a mountain that rises up from the sea floor so that there are chambers completely sealed off from ocean water. And," a tearful swell closed her throat again, "my friend Vatu is here. I never could have expected."

"I'm happy for you." Andle never tired of stories about the Mingal and her amazing skills. Transforming, going without food or water for long stretches, adjusting body temperature.

"There's something else." Yanda so needed a friend to talk to about all that was happening. Yes, Vatu was there, but she had her chum Alyena. Yanda and Andle had confided everything over recent months. "Tenali didn't desert me. He's hunting for Seiti."

"Have you told him she could be with the Blaz?" Andle asked.

"I've not been in touch with him." She knew she'd told Andle that.

"You should try to get his mom to reach him."

Yanda thought, then said, "It's time to contact Tlalit and Merne." Merne and her son Tenali had gone long periods out of touch, when he was still angry that the Neyna would not reach out to the Neyla for help fight the colonizers who still threatened Shalt, the Elves' loving and powerful stone.

"I'll see if they've been in contact with Tenali." Yanda watched her little boy, not two yet, letting the gerbil-like animal crawl up his arm, giggling when its whiskers tickled his neck. She drank in the sight of him, pressing her wrist-bot to the screen to record a vid. "Kiss, kiss, baby. I love you soooo sooo much."

"I love you this much." He held up his arms wide.

"I'll be home soon. You take care of Andle, okay?" Yanda's voice broke.

"I will, Me-me. We go *sutati* tonight." He beamed.

*Sutati* was a gathering they held just before breaking camp, to keep up their spirits as they left yet another place they'd called home.

Yanda's heart squeezed at not being able to be there to keep him safe. But she smiled. "That'll be fun. Only one sweet waffle."

Zami wrinkled his nose at her.

Andle leaned forward. "We'll go underground first. We'll be fine. Sandor will stay close, help me make sure this little guy's safe and happy."

"He's always happy with you and your critters." Yanda smiled, though the heartache wouldn't stop, knowing she'd soon have to end the connection. "It's good Sandor's helping. But doesn't he have to get back to Skarth?"

Yanda said the name of the city where she'd been an impressive upcoming surgeon, where her apartment was now a strange and complicated base for a counter-movement, though it was hard to tell where it placed her. Did she love the movement? Is it what she'd always hoped for? Or were they enemies to her, right within her home walls, in her tall building, aerial trains shooting by, high above crowded streets? A large bittersweet cloud hovered around that city's name for Yanda. It was where her first dreams had been aimed, brought to an abrupt end: her coming-of-age years, her growing awareness of the bigotry that controlled her planet.

"He's taken a leave of absence." Andle turned away and Yanda heard commotion in the background. "I'll get back to you—"

The line went dead.

Yanda felt dread. She stood, ready to track down Merne and Tlalit and get on their ship, back to Alland, back to her son.

Andle flickered into view once again. "I'll be brief. Take care of the business you went for. Get help finding Seiti. You know we always come out okay." The screen went dark.

Yanda's stomach roiled with terror, choices torn into cutting shards within her.

A wave smashed against the walls surrounding the tech room and she jumped. Tide must be rising. The room darkened. Small windows at the tops of the curving walls showed foam, then solid water. She felt suddenly tired of this wet world.

Rushing to the door where Kalden had exited, she tapped lightly, waited, then tested the handle. The door slid open. A blackened room with tall banks of flickering lights, obscured any clear vision until her eyes adjusted. Kalden and others were at stations with strange structures on their heads. Kalden lifted off his headwear, flipped switches, and turned to Yanda. Swiftly he crossed the room and nudged her out, closing the door silently behind.

"Finished?" he asked in a low voice.

"Got cut off," she said, a sob unexpectedly rising into her throat.

"I'm sorry." He gently took her elbow. "The council will see you now."

Yanda gasped, fingers pressed to her lips. She hadn't expected it so soon. Was there some preparation she should have? Would it be like the Neyna Circle? That was powerful and she had needed some initiatory instruction. In fact, she'd felt something change in her once she entered that Circle. This was not a small thing to take on. Yet...if the Neyla could help get her daughter back.

Why had she thought they might be able to? As she followed Kalden to the lower level, she tried to remember what her thinking had been. Just that Ash-don was as powerful as Shalt, but not part of the Neyna, not connected with Zamani. She'd felt the Neyla Circle's immense energy, and when the two Circle's joined, they defeated Krid's army.

To her surprise, she found herself in the hall outside Mnenu's office.

Kalden knocked.

Mnenu yanked open the door. His smile was brief, a quick lift of mouth corners. He wore a long robe now, of dark tones. Standing tall, with a grave expression, he took her breath away. "Come." He gestured and started down the hall.

Yanda followed. Kalden remained behind.

They turned right, descending down a corridor that seemed to wind deep into the mountain, for sounds of the sea became muffled.

If they slowed, she felt throbbing under her feet, as she'd detected in his office. The further she went, the more it intensified.

This had to be Shalt's sister stone. Or brother? Ash-don. The impact grew until she drew to a stop, hand on one wet cave wall.

As she'd done on the approach to Shalt, she dropped to her knees, nausea gripping her.

Mnenu knelt by her, his hand pressed to her face. She stared at the floor, trying to master the bile that threatened to rise.

He moved her head gently so she looked at him. She winced at first as he drew her into a close mind connection. "Let me help," he said into her thoughts without speaking.

For a moment, she fought such intense sharing with this man who had at times rubbed her the wrong way. It was too much, too sudden.

But he was bringing Ash-don's resonances into balance, attuning her to the powerful vibrations.

Slowly, her stomach settled. Her body thrummed. The reverberations resounding through her now felt exhilarating. Both Mnenu's hands cupped her face.

With a grunt, she pushed off the wall and climbed to standing.

He let go of her face, one hand slipping to her elbow. "You steady now?"

She nodded, breathless. "Yeah. Much better." His touch on her arm sent volts of electricity. Not in a bad way. She bounced on the balls of her feet as they walked to the end of the dark hallway, lit only by low-glowing wall sconces.

Through immense double doors, they entered a round

antechamber with thick carpet and stunning paneled walls. Light came from glowing strips woven into panels inset at intervals around them.

Yanda stared up at rounded ceiling that glowed more intensely where the light panels came together, coalescing at the peak.

Mnenu held out a robe to her. "It's a formality that you wear this."

She dropped her arms into the wide hanging sleeves and pulled it shut around her. He helped her fasten brocaded ties, letting silken tassels fall to the front, and straightened the high collar to stand part up behind her head. She wished she could see herself.

Mnenu grinned. "Let me be your mirror." He gave her a picture of herself, as he saw her.

She grew shy as a glow shone in his eyes, conveying approval. Well, she'd admired him as well, seeing him in his dramatic robe.

"Shall we?" His expression turned sober as he crossed the room, pulling her after him by her hand, and pushed open a tall narrow door set into a deep alcove on the far side.

They stepped into darkness. Cold wind rushed at them from all sides, along with the sounds of pounding surf from far below.

Yanda shivered, glad of the heavy robe. Slowly her eyes adjusted to phosphorescence on distant walls of a massive sea cave. Bit by bit, she made out forms, deep grey against charcoal. Mnenu led her to one of the looming shapes: a tall seat carved from the stone of this ledge.

She recognized the arrangement: like the Neynu circle in the crystal pyramid, called Vashal, but here the stone chairs were molded from the sea-cliff itself.

She climbed steps carved into the side and took her place in the indention that formed a chair. As she settled, warmth seemed to come from beneath her. The vast cavern, black as night, stretched around her. Eleven others on high seats circled an immense hole. Below, the sea churned and crashed. A rounded sphere separated the waters.

She hadn't seen where Mnenu went.

She closed her eyes and laid her head back against hard, cold stone.

The presence of others did not immediately fill her mind, perhaps because she didn't know the Neyla well. When she became aware of them, their mind vibrations were different from the Forest Elves. As sea shifters, they thought, in ways, like sea creatures. She noticed Mnenu among them, his high seat some distance from hers.

The Great Stone, Ash-don, spoke. It may have spoken long before but the ideas had to come into her heart and cells before her brain. "You have need of me" was how she understood its message.

"I am humbled to be in your presence." It seemed right for Yanda to say that.

Approval rippled through the minds of the Circle.

"I don't deserve your attention," she went on.

A series of hiccups nearly threw her from her seat. With soul-knowing, she realized what this was. Ash-Don laughing! Then a flood of picture-ideas paraded through her consciousness. She knew, in the way the Fugitives had formed a hive-mind, that all the Circle saw these with her: drawn from her home planet, leaving her six-year-old daughter behind, her captivity with the Ten Fems, working with Shalt to draw back its pieces from across space, finally her immense cry when she learned her daughter may have been kidnapped by Blaz traders.

Yanda heaved a sob as she suffered through these memories.

How could the Stone of the Neyla know her life? What about her infancy, her birth parents abandoning her on Alland? Had the Stone seen those as well?

"You are not insignificant, Surgeon, Through-Seer, Xentu daughter." When Ash-don, spoke, it was as though she were a mountain vein, and the energies poured into her, herself part of the soil and metals, rivers and sea foam, stone itself.

"Can you help me find Seiti?" Yanda asked, her heartfelt request channeling through the circle and gaining resonance, expanding in its force.

"You must give me her essence. Can you do that?" Ash-don asked.

"I'm not sure. I can try." Yanda thought he meant convey her to the Stone so that he could sense her anywhere in the universe. Was she capable of such a thing?

She need not have worried. The Stone showed her the way. Seiti was suddenly fully present in her mind, as if she dreamed. Her daughter's essence, her voice, her breath, permeated Yanda's entire being.

# CHAPTER

## 20

**W**hen the sensation receded, Yanda let out an agonized cry as if she'd just discovered her loss for the first time, grasping to have her daughter's presence back.

Her connection with the Circle ended abruptly. She heard footsteps. Mnenu climbed the high stone chair to hold her.

"I'm sorry," she sobbed into his shoulder. "I did it wrong. Did I hurt the Circle? I shouldn't have broken off like that."

"No, no. Emotion is part of all of us. Even the Circle." He brushed back her hair from her face with a warm, gentle hand. "When I feel this way, I need to swim. Deep and long. Would you come with me?"

She stared at him. "I can't swim underwater like you."

"Would you like to be able to?" he asked, as if it were so simple.

Others walked past them, in low-voiced conversations.

A few reached up and patted her arm. They sent mind-messages of comfort, which she read easily now. All were congratulatory.

What had she done? "Why do they congratulate me?" she asked Mnenu.

He let out a guffaw. "Come." He scrambled down, and reached back for her.

She held his hand to descend the slick, black stone stairs, though she was starting to notice that these Neyla boots gripped the surfaces as though she had salamander feet.

When she walked onto the granite shelf, he tousled her hair. "Do you think just anyone can step directly into this Circle and communicate with Ash-don? Most could not even mind-meld with the Circle, much less with the Stone. You have powers, woman."

Elation washed over her, though also caution; too much hubris can get you into trouble, or at least crash you later. She knew this all too well.

They started across the dark surface that thundered with the sea below, following the rest, before she realized Mnenu held her hand. It was dark but even so, she grew conscious of what it might mean to others.

When they stepped into the vestibule, he let go. The others were hanging their robes on the twelve hooks. She slipped hers off and Mnenu hung it with the rest. Those of the Circle, with whom she'd just shared minds, chattered animatedly as they left.

"What did you mean, would I like to be able to swim underwater like you?" she asked cautiously, as they exited in their turn, but down a different corridor. She thought she could easily get lost down there.

"I think you might learn to shift so you could."

"Vatu can shift. But I never have. What makes you think I'd be able to?" Annoyance and excitement stirred in Yanda.

"Some of the Xentu have that ability," he answered, studying her.

"Wouldn't it have shown up by now?" she asked.

"Not necessarily. It could be latent. I may be able to help you trigger it."

They had turned another corner and heard the sea. Through an archway, they entered a sea cave dotted with steaming pools, enjoyed by numerous Elves and visitors.

"There's one in particular that has very rich waters. We use it for healing." Mnenu led the way along a ledge and up narrow well-worn stairs. They squeezed through a crevice into a small, dark chamber formed of natural stone. A central pool reflected colors from glowing iridescent walls, primarily midnight blue but with brighter crimson and gold shades.

"This is gorgeous," Yanda stared at the colors.

Mnenu grinned as he stripped off his clothes. "Come in."

Self-conscious at first, she slipped off the loaned outfit, stashed it in a dry place, and tested the water, then lowered herself onto a naturally formed bench under the surface.

Mnenu took her hand and tugged.

She sank in deeper. "Feels good." Her red-brown hair spread out on the surface of the water.

"It's regenerative." He dunked under, then came up, face next to hers.

"How deep is it?" Yanda kept her hand connected with the stone side.

"No one knows. You won't find the bottom."

"Oh wow. That's…" She hugged closer to the side. "…a little unnerving."

"Come. There's a shelf at the back. Very safe." He pushed off and, with two strokes, arrived where the pool curved into a hollow in the cave wall.

She followed, keeping a hand to the edge. When she reached the curve in the pool, his strong arms pulled her into an embrace. They sat in a scooped-out portion of the pool next to a low waterfall.

After their recent mind-melding with the great Stone and the Circle, the connection remained and she found it easy to be drawn closer. Suspicion pushing its way in, she laughed and shoved against his chest. "Is this where you seduce people?"

"Actually, sex would make it easier." His expression was neutral as he slid her to sit on his thigh, snugged into his side.

She chuckled, still holding back, studying his face.

Water dripped from stray hairs on his forehead, and caught like pearls on his eyelashes.

The water was perfectly hot and relaxing. She eased back and floated just above the reassuring lap of stone under them.

"I'm serious," he said, sliding his arm over her stomach, pulling her close and kissing her. It felt good, the slippery water, their skin together.

He sat up cross legged, back curved into the wall of the pool, and lifted her into his lap. They kissed, long and lingering. Heat smoldered in Yanda, from belly to groin, speeding up her heart. Her hand ran along his smooth leaf-shaped ear.

Speaking against her lips, Mnenu said, "One way to trigger a latent power is orgasm."

Yanda pushed back and stared at him, then with a guffaw, said, "That's the best line I've ever heard." When his expression didn't change, she said, "No way. That's…ridiculous."

He gently moved her legs around him, his hardness between them. Their eyes met, hers still twinkling, a chuckle formed on her lips. He joined minds with her, like in the Circle but more intimate. He gave into her thoughts the sensation of swimming in the sea, breathing underwater, gliding with the *tesu*, undulating, the lower body propelling a leap out of the water.

They shot into the air, together, as one. At that moment, he eased into her. They moved together. Her mind was half out at sea, half in the act of making love.

And then they *were* in the sea, swimming in long powerful strokes.

The water was cold and deep and dark, above and below her. For a moment, Yanda panicked, heart racing, skin prickling with dread.

Mnenu kept his arm around her as they shot through the water. She grabbed his arm to get his attention, shook her head, running out of air. He put his mouth on hers, holding her tight. "I'm breathing into you. Let your lungs expand, I'm going to slowly let you take over. Let your gills work."

After a moment, his warm mouth left hers. Steeling herself, she searched for a sense of oxygen coming in. And for the first time in her life, did not live by drawing breath.

"Why am I not cold?" she asked in mind-speak.

"Because you're a thing of the sea now." He laughed in her mind, and she saw his eyes sparkling, protected by nictating membranes that closed and opened from the sides.

"Let's go back." Exhilarated, she was also exhausted.

"Just one jump," he cajoled.

Their bodies gyrated together as they surged toward the surface. Yanda realized her legs worked as if they were boneless, all muscle. They broke the surface and shot upward.

Before they plunged back in, she caught a glimpse of the sparkling blanket of stars overhead. Still entwined, they dropped into the sea, and then were back in the cavern, in the warmth of the pool.

Yanda looked down at herself. Her legs were normal, separate, with bones. "Was that just a spirit journey?" she asked. It would be a disappointment, though this had been sudden, not something she'd thought about, longed for, even known was possible.

"Not at all." He touched her sides where the gills had been.

Awareness bloomed; her body was changed.

"Wow." So much had happened that day. She'd talked to her son, taken part in the powerful Circle with the Neyla, communed with Ash-don, and transformed into a sea creature. It was hard to take it all in, yet she needed to. "Do you think Ash-don got enough to search for my daughter? Could you tell?"

"I think so, yes." He pulled her into a warm hug, lying in the shallow bowl formed by the pool so they were mostly submerged.

They lay that way a while, then climbed out.

Yanda wished she had a towel, and in that instant, her new ability kicked in; she was dry, even her hair. "That's handy," she said, pulling on her one-piece outfit.

Mnenu winked at her as he tugged on his pants.

Soon they were walking out among the pools in the outer cave.

"Do you know the way to Vatu's rooms?" she asked.

"Of course."

Yanda was keenly aware of Mnenu beside her along dark hallways. When a wave crashed against the stone wall next to them, where before she would have jumped, now she retained some of her undersea senses, an echo of the sea depths remained, a new knowing clung to her. She needed no float globe to illuminate their path; her night-sight lit up the darkest corners; she wondered if her eyes glowed in the dark.

Their hands brushed. Part of her longed to discuss the changes in her, yet, more profoundly, she wanted to ponder and feel for herself: What would it mean to her life, that she could transform into a sea creature? Maybe not useful on Alland, but what about when she visited Mingal? What else might she be able to shift into?

He had brought this about. How had he known?

If he detected her questions, he too decided to hold off on speaking. He held her hand until they arrived in the delicately intricate vestibule of Vatu's quarters, well lit by tiny twinkle globes showing the seashell encrusted ribs of the room.

"We're here." Yanda took in a breath, turning to Mnenu.

His dark eyes penetrated hers, mind-deep.

Yanda's chest rose and fell as her heart raced.

Mnenu's echoed hers and he drew her to him with large, warm hands. Their lips met in a soft kiss, then crushed together.

Yanda heard voices inside, and her hands came up between them but did not push. She wanted to sink into this man-elf and never let go.

His lips slid away along her cheek to her ear. "I want

much more of this. Much, much more of you."

Shivers ran down her spine.

He eased back and his face was serious, hungry, intense.

Vatu's voice in her mind teased, "Are you coming in or what?"

Mnenu's thumb brushed her jaw as he straightened, separating from her. "Are you lovers?" he asked, clearly meaning Vatu.

That question made her pause. "Sisters of the soul," she answered.

Mnenu chewed his lip, pensive. His eyes were far off for a moment. The he said, smiling, "Get some sleep."

The mother in her reinserted itself as her hands dropped from him. "Do you think there will be answers tomorrow?"

"Tomorrow will be a very big day. What all it will bring, I can't know."

She turned toward the door, but looked back. He stood still, facing her, and gave her a nod. She raised a hand, then entered Vatu's chambers, watching him until the door shut.

"Tell all." Vatu was curled on her bed, chin on fists, in comfy nightclothes.

Alyena sat against the wall, quilt over her legs, eyes eager.

"All?" Yanda asked, a mischievous twinkle in her eyes, as she climbed to the upper room. She'd never known Vatu to take a lover and they'd never spoken of such things.

Once she'd changed into a borrowed nightgown, she came back down and told them about her day: meeting with Mnenu, talking to Zami, connecting with the Circle of Ash-Don.

"I transformed, *Vati*." She called her by the nickname she'd sometimes used during their long captivity together. "I swam in the sea, with gills and boneless legs. I had night sight, and could intuit what was in the water around me. I wasn't afraid." Her breaths came shallow and quick with her excitement.

Vatu was sitting straight up in her bed now, staring at Yanda. "Mnenu did that for you? Helped you find your shifter?" She threw her arms around her in a hug. They laughed, cried, hiccoughed. Then Vatu grew somber. "I wonder if I could have done that for you."

Yanda hadn't brought up the sexual part of the process. She shrugged. "It doesn't matter. I have it now."

Vatu turned to Alyena. "We can all swim together, explore."

Alyena grinned and yawned. "Yay." She got up to leave.

Vatu laughed. "We've had a long day." She narrowed her eyes, inquisition-style. "What's going on with Mnenu and you? I'm thinking not so much animosity?"

"Don't go nosing around in my head, you." Yanda shook Vatu's knee. "Good night, you two." She climbed the stairs again to her loft-room and dropped into bed.

Vatu extinguished lights.

In the silence and dark, Yanda became aware of the waves splashing high windows. One of the moons—the bluest, Shalit—filtered in through ocean spray, striking the upper walls. What had Mnenu meant, that it would be a big day tomorrow? Might she see her daughter? Seiti was two years older than when Yanda had been abducted. She'd missed that part of her little girl's life. She willed her mind to think positive. Maybe she was taking the right steps to get her back. At least she wasn't just sitting in the rebel camp on Alland.

Yanda thought of her son. For the first time, she had missed a few weeks of his life.

Tenali came into her mind. He'd left to search for her daughter, and here she was, taking another love. Not that anything had ever been promised between them, or even articulated, about the future, about anything lasting.

He was the one who'd alerted Merne and Tlalit of the possible sighting of Seiti, and the presence of Blaz traders nearby. Now he was off trying to find her little girl and rescue her. But he'd never tried to contact her. Probably hadn't dared, for fear of giving away her location. That's what she'd told herself, over and over again. They'd been so close, shared so much about their early lives, about their unknown origins—something neither of them spoke of often. While living with the rebels of Alland, she'd expected to get some word from him, then heard he'd left. She'd been hurt and tried to cut him out of her heart. Now she couldn't even remain angry with him.

Maybe she could be the one to make contact, with Shalt or Ash-don's help. Or use her new AI ability. Lying in bed, she sent her mind out, casting her net wide.

Ash-don spoke to her—very gently for a massive power stone: "You should be sleeping. We can do this searching together."

Startled, she pulled back into the sphere of her mind. How should she answer the Great Stone? "Did I disturb you?"

"I don't sleep." There was that emanation she'd learned was the stone's chuckle. "Don't worry. As long as you are in my realm, I will make sure you are not detected."

"I thought I *was* being undetectable," she conveyed, ruefully.

"For most, yes. I can teach you to hide even from me."

Yanda sought her best cocoon state. "How's this?"

Amusement again. "That's fine, human child. Now rest."

She no longer felt the Stone. As she emptied her mind, her memories drifted to Mnenu in the hot pool. She'd known what he knew, saw what he saw, while feeling her own feelings. All her love-making with Elven men had been like that, shared in spirit and soul as well as mind. But the physical dimensions of what she and Mnenu shared—when they'd leapt, body and spirit, out of the sea, bodies entwined, sleek as seals, building power together, soaring between water and sky, part of the elements—now that she had no fear, she knew only wonder.

Carried by those thoughts, she slept.

# CHAPTER

# 21

**M**orning dawned, loud with storm winds, thunder, and crashing waves. Yanda dressed quickly, amazed to have woken before the Mingals. She remembered the *swapan*—a small thin device Kalden had given her—and adhered it to her inner arm as she left Vatu's quarters.

Hurrying down the hall, she held her thumb to the second-skin disc and thought the code Kalden had given her so she could contact him if she needed to.

She saw him in her mind's eye, grinning.

"Coming to breakfast?" he asked.

"Yes." That was an afterthought. "I wondered if I might speak to my son again this morning."

"It might be hard today," he responded.

Yanda's heart sank. "Okay, see you soon." She remembered her way using a mnemonic mind-map to recall the maze of tunnels to the dining hall, a practice that was getting easier due to her new spatial awareness.

Pushing through the double doors, her eyes rested on a most unexpected sight; seated at the long table facing her were Merne, Tlalit, and Zamani, her son's father, three of the most important Neyna Elves. What were they doing here in Zotoul? They never came here. She'd only seen the Elven groups together during Withum Festival when all the Elven folk renewed their psychic meld by breathing the pollen of the Withum flower. It was a truce time.

She'd been trying to avoid this encounter. Her stomach churned as she considered slipping back out. But Zamani spotted her and stood abruptly, pushing back his chair to give the slight bow of the wood Elves. He wore elegant clothing she'd only seen at special occasions: a green almost-black velvet robe, trimmed in twining strands of ice blue and moss green. He made a handsome figure, tall, well built, ageless.

Lion-eyed Merne looked up from deep conversation with Tlalit. The tiny primate, Tuk-Tuk, perched on her shoulder, and Yanda's heart squeezed, thinking of how her son loved the little creature. She must tie up her business here and get back to him.

Tlalit's apricot hair, peaked as usual at the top of her head, cresting above myriad earrings in her translucent, leaf-shaped ears of melon-yellow.

Yanda swallowed, wondering what this meant—the three of them in delegation—as she made her way to them and touched foreheads with each, then sat in the chair Zamani offered.

Many eyes in the hall were on their small group.

Zamani leaned toward her and offered, in his rich low voice, "I'll bring you something to eat, unless you want to choose your own."

"Oh, anything is fine," she said.

Zamani returned soon with a full plate. Some looked delectable and familiar, some wildly not, like a yellow-gold puddle with large round lumps. She edged around it with a mother-of-pearl spoon and finally dipped into a dark mound, bracing herself for Zamani to demand where their son was.

Zamani picked up his fork but held it mid-air over his plate. "You came to the Neyla for help," he said, calmly, as if commenting on the weather. Under his words ran currents filled with tension and censure.

Yanda had prepared for such a moment, but hadn't expected it in the Neyla undersea city. "Yes. Merne and Tlalit reported to me that my daughter may have been sighted on Shagal. I thought—" She stopped. All the reasons she'd constructed escaped her as she looked into his swirling Elven eyes. She said, instead, "Shalt told me nothing of my daughter's disappearance. I arrived home after nearly two years away and she was gone. Had left home, searching for me." Yanda felt the real story tumbling out, along with tears she hadn't known had risen until they fell on toast coated with sea-fruit jelly. She swiped her face. Zamani had this effect, making her want to tell all, tell the truth. She knew he likely had a very full report from daughter, Merne, anyway.

"And Zami is where, exactly?" Zamani picked up a slice of seaweed pastry and tore it in half, then in quarters, then in eighths.

"Safe."

"With rebels hiding in Outer Alland." His eyebrow angled upward. "Safe, you say."

She'd never been questioned like this by him before. But Elves seldom had children; therefore, young ones were considered a sacred part of the Neyna people. Out of the corner of her eye, Yanda saw Mnenu step to the other side of their table.

"We should join the Circle soon," Mnenu said.

Relief poured into her, along with a large dose of guilt as she tore her eyes from Zamani's compelling stare.

With consummate grace, all three Neyna stood, pushing their plates deliberately to the center of the table. Yanda followed suit.

No one spoke as they made their way down the halls to the round entry giving onto the sea shelf above Ash-Don. All dressed in the thick robes to join the Circle.

Yanda dreaded being in the Circle with these Neyna.

Five of the seats were left empty for them. All felt very ceremonial and weighty. As Mnenu led Yanda to her stone perch, he briefly touched her hand. The air seemed to crackle around her briefly before he left her for his own seat, fifteen feet away. The sea crashed thunderously beneath them in the storm.

Maybe it would be just as well, she thought, to get everything out in the open in a mind-meld where she was not alone but had the full Neyla Circle with her, as tension pinged through her insides.

Ash-don's powerful thoughts took a moment to establish coherence in her mind. The force of a dozen minds coming together with hers surged in with a different tone. Maybe it was just her nerves over the Neyna's sudden visit. Unlike before, a *solutio*—alchemical dissolving—threatened.

Then Ash-don's thoughts took form. "It has been long since a Neyna delegation has joined us in Tsatari."

She knew by being in this hive of minds that Tsatari was the ancient, sacred name for this cavern.

"We were honored with the Xentu daughter in our

Circle one planet-turn ago," Ash-don went on intoning into their minds, "and now, three Neyna of the most ancient bloodline…"

Yanda sensed there was some challenge embedded in the seemingly celebratory comments. Xentu daughter. They all identified this part of her that signified nothing to her, yet was valued greatly by them.

Ash-don got to the point. "What brings you to us after so much time?"

"I felt her cry for help," Zamani said. "From Alland."

Yanda had a picture of him in her mind, of the tall Elf-man dwarfed before a moon-sized stone that stretched beneath as well as far beyond them.

"As did many of us," Ash-don replied.

"Then I learned she was here."

"And you thought you'd come to help her." What was Ash-don's meaning? The Stone seemed to rumble.

After a moment, Zamani said, "I'm sorry we've been silent so long."

This was probably a historic moment, Yanda thought: An apology from the Neyna leader.

"It was Yanda who asked us to join together the last time, as I recall, to defeat Kridenit and his forces." Ash-don seemed to miss nothing and remember everything.

"That is true." Zamani did not hide his memory of the scene at the dinner when Tenali begged them to consider joining forces with Ash-don's Circle to bring back Shalt's pieces from across the universe, so the Stone would have wholeness and full power again.

If they'd listened to Tenali sooner, I might not have had to be pulled away from my daughter and, ultimately, lost her, Yanda thought. But then, I wouldn't have my son. I would never have known Zami.

A tremor ran through the Circle. With dismay, Yanda realized her lapse into her own thoughts had threatened the integrity of the Circle. Horrified, she concentrated with all her might on the mind-share.

Ash-don focused on her. As on the previous day, she was the focal point, alone, naked, battered by the enormity of a Moon's mind.

"I'm sorry," she said. "My mind wandered."

"You are young and new to this Circle. And you have many worries."

That was nice of the Stone. Was another shoe about to fall? "Thank you."

"Your daughter is gone from you. Why?"

Was this a trick question? Like a lesson? "I was drawn away from her. At the time, I had no idea how to work with mind powers. Not that I know so much now." Only humility would do. "I heard only Shalt, could think of nothing else, until I was on the Lark, captured, my means of communicating with my family taken from me."

"For over a year—in your terms, similar to this planet's turn around our star—you had no contact with your daughter. When you went to look for her, she'd left the planet of Alland."

"That's right. Krid threatened that if I tried to reach out to her, he would hurt my family."

"And now you know nothing of her whereabouts."

"Nothing but a possible sighting on Shagal." By this time, Yanda floated in a sort of chaos. Was she down on the rocks below the shelf, with Ash-don? Or did she still sit on the stone seat? She had no idea. Ocean spray mingled with tears on her face. She was neither warm nor cold, pure meld-mind, and wretched. "Do you know where she is?"

"I do not know where Seiti is."

The Stone knew her daughter's name. Or did her own mind fill in the gaps? What was this Stone's sentience, anyway? A devilish doubt filled her, as hope dashed against the rock.

"I think you do," Ash-don's thought rolled through her like a tank.

*  *  *

Yanda struggled to open her eyes. Her head ached. She lay on a settee in a small room, walls lined in heavy fabric, unsure if she'd walked her there, or was carried, unconscious.

Mnenu knelt beside her. "How do you feel?"

"Can't you read my mind?" She'd grown suddenly testy, suspicious of mind-powers, wrung out by the encounter with Zamani, and then Ash-don.

"Not unless invited to," he said, wounded.

Is that your ego hurt, or a formal statement of a tenet? she wondered, having no store of empathy in her final disappointment.

He took her hand. "Ash-don did not say he cannot find Seiti. The Stone does not *know* where she is. Now."

"But he...it...said I know. What does that mean? That I've known all along but am holding back?" She pulled herself into a tight, miserable ball, snot and sea-spray wet on the seat.

Mnenu was silent a moment, then said, "It might mean your daughter's not showing up in any known place. Maybe it's a place only you *can* know."

She raised her head, shoved tangled hair aside, stared at him, then scooted upright on the lounge. "Is that possible? And what would that mean?"

"It might be. What do you know of your people?"

"What does that have to do with it?" Yanda snapped, so tired of the Xentu business. The Elves seemed to worship the very word. Every time she heard it, she felt more orphaned, a waif without a home, no real parentage, no sense of herself. She'd come to her powers by stumbling on them, had never had training until she'd been a prisoner—pregnant and far from her home planet.

Mnenu took her hand and ran a fingertip along the back.

She shivered. That wasn't fair. Did he know what that did to her? But he wasn't looking at her face and his expression conveyed no intention of seduction. When his eyes met hers, she saw profound sorrow.

His mouth turned up at the corners but his eyes bore into hers. "Don't you want to know?"

Do I want to know who my parents were? After a lifetime of wondering? When I'm lightyears away from my little boy, and who knows how far from my daughter—a little girl who may be in the hands of torturers, slavers? She took her hand away and balled both fists into her stomach. "My supposed Xentu heritage is not the first thing on my mind."

"But it might be important, for finding Seiti. It might hold answers. Where would your daughter go, and could anyone else be involved?" He peered into her face.

"What do you mean?"

# CHAPTER

# 22

H e heaved a sigh. "Xentu blood is not common. And the Xentu, from what I know, do not let their own go lightly."

"Well, they dumped *me*. And how do you even know that? Anyway, what makes you all think I'm Xentu?"

"Yandawi. You don't understand. I've not only been in these seas." He searched around, as though ways of expressing himself might appear in the air. "There are not many Xentu. It's a small race. And the members are like legend. Your name is part of the legend." He got up and joined her on the cushions.

She scooted to make room for him.

"I have traveled and studied, you know." His expression was both proud and defensive.

Why was he saying this, as if contradicting something she'd said? Was it a thought he'd caught in her mind? She *had* assumed he'd only ever been in his Elven world of Zotoul. In fact, it *was* hard to picture him anywhere else. "Where have you been?" she asked.

He laughed. "You can't picture me at a university, can you?" He shoved dark stray hairs back from his eyes. "Why? Don't I look suited for scholarship?" He glanced down at himself.

"It's not that." She shrugged. "I just didn't know. What does any of that tell you about my suspected Xentu blood?"

He wrapped an arm around her shoulders and drew her close. "I'll tell you all. If you want to know."

"All?" She teased, buying time. Her guests, Zamani, Merne and Tlalit, weighed on her mind. They'd be waiting. She dreaded further conversation with Zamani, more anger and reprimand, but it could not be avoided forever.

"They're gone," Mnenu said.

She leaned away, studying his face. "Back to Rotoul?"

"Mm-hmm." His thumb caressed her cheek.

It couldn't be that easy. She frowned. "They were hardly here. What happened?"

"I don't know. But we'll see them again soon enough."

She quirked a quizzical brow.

"Withum," he replied as if she'd forgotten the most obvious of things.

"Is that soon?" She remembered well the yearly festival when all Elven minds melded in one-love.

"Very soon."

"By the way, I can picture you anywhere. I just hadn't."

"Oh. That makes me feel better. Would you like to see my apartment?"

Yanda laughed at the sudden change of topic.

"You could call your son from there," he added.

Yanda perked up immediately. Then, at his wounded laugh, she wished she'd been more subtle, but he pulled her into a deep, warm kiss.

She turned into him, moving her legs over his lap. "You're going to show me your apartment, eh?"

His brows went up, mock-contrite. "I thought you might…be curious."

"Oh, I am." Her expression was casual, teasing, as her heart pounded. "I did wonder if it's similar to Vatu's."

Mnenu pulled her to standing. "Then you will see it."

\* \* \*

She couldn't have anticipated the splendor of Mnenu's wing. Every part highlighted views of the sea, either under it or looking out over. Tall narrow windows angled toward light, ascending to peaks above. Deep, rich tones imitated sea caverns yet with refinement and artistry accentuating nature. Carvings and wall sconces resembled sea ferns and palms, sea horses and corals.

"Oh," she gasped, turning around to take it in, exploring the several rooms—his own kitchen, living room, library.

"Come." A beautiful panel, camouflaged into the wall, slid open at the press of his hand.

She followed him into a cylindrical chamber. When the door hissed shut, they rose. Dark walls turned light as they shot up into a tower, above the surf.

"Tricky," she said, gazing at a vast sea stretching to the horizon.

"That's the least of it," Mnenu said, as they stepped out into the tower room. He typed code and a panel lit up. A floor covering slid open and then descended into a dark room.

Instrumentation glowed softly on the walls. At a touch on a panel, soft seats dropped from insets.

"Sit." Mnenu took his own cushioned perch, next to hers. "You have a code for your friend's channel?" His hand hovered over the panel.

"Kalden took it from my head. I guess he knew where to look." She felt silly. "Not a very reliable system if I had to do it myself."

"Let's see about that." Mnenu slid his knees around hers and pressed his hands to her temples. After a silent moment, he took his hands away, pensive. "You were taught to hide thoughts, right?"

"By Shouma, yes."

"I've heard of her. Impressive woman."

"Yes." A pang raced through her, missing her mentor and friend. Shouma had been more like a mother to her than the woman she called Mom who'd raised her.

"But never taught to save information safely, to draw on later? Something like numbers, complex names or wordings?" he asked.

"No. We have implants on my world. I never chose to embed, and Krid probably would have torn them out. But plenty of arm patches and devices to hold information."

"You don't need that. I can teach you more later, but for now, let me show you the part of your mind where the code is." Mnenu again had his hands to her head, locking minds with her.

A beautiful chest of drawers unfolded from nothing, and a row of numbers shifted to the front. She typed on a keypad he'd swiveled between them, then let the numbers slip into a drawer labeled "Code".

"You can decorate as you see fit," he said, chuckling.

"I gave it a motif I like."

"Okay." Yanda heard Andle's voice and turned to the screen on the wall next to her.

"I'll let you be private." Mnenu crossed the room and, putting on headphones, opened a terminal of his own.

With bubbling love filling her stomach, Yanda saw her son's little face appear next to Andle. She pulled on headphones hanging by the screen, then decided to put a silent sphere around herself, longing to mind-speak. That was their best form of communication.

Zami grinned at her, stroking a fluffy baby animal in his toddler arms. "Yes, I'm being good. I help Andle." His lips hadn't moved.

He'd received her thought! "How do you help her?" she asked, again in mind-speak.

"Feed the chickens, and clean. And make food. I made my bed this morning."

He was so capable for such a young age. Her throat ached.

She glanced at Mnenu who seemed oblivious. What did he think of the silence? Yet it felt private, perfect. Could she and Zami reach each other without the tech connection now that they'd formed this channel? She'd try to find out, later.

"You have ocean there," he thought to her. "You swam in it, deep, deep."

"I did. I'll bring you here to swim, too." She thought about him learning to transform, swimming with the *tesu*. Longing to touch his soft skin, to breathe in his scent, she reached toward the screen.

"When you come home?" he asked, finally showing a tremulous lip.

"Very soon, darling. I'm trying to get your sister back."

"I know."

Andle's face appeared next to his. "We probably shouldn't keep this connection too long."

"Why did you have to move camp? What happened?"

The connection dropped and the screen went blank.

Yanda stared at it, willing them to be safe. She glanced at Mnenu, who turned, pushed back his headphones, and came to her, taking in the black screen.

"They had to go," she lied. Why lie? Because their disappearance accented the danger she might have left for her tiny boy?

He held out a hand to her. "We are called back to the council."

"So soon?" Yanda asked, her mind still agitating over the drop in the connection to her son.

Did this mean Ash-don had found her daughter? Or the reverse. The Stone would dash her hopes. Eager and filled with dread, she stood.

Mnenu ran a finger up a strip on the wall and they descended back into sea rock, the light disappearing from outside, only interior now.

Peripherally she wondered what everything was made of. They used no metal, mined for nothing.

* * *

They again put on the robes and joined ten others on the rock seats, the high domed cavern filled with the sound of crashing waves. The storm had receded but the ocean still churned. She tried to catch a glimpse of Ash-don but dared not step close to the edge of the shelf that held them, circling the massive hole.

This time, as the seat warmed to her body, the melding of minds came easily. She felt the others welcome her, some familiar, a few new to her.

And then the fiercely intense presence of the Stone beneath them made its presence known.

She didn't always feel sure she understood the Stone's intent. It was not as clear to her as Shalt, but then she'd been drawn by Shalt. She'd lain on the moon-sized stone's surface and felt her cells attune to its resonances.

Then she did understand. With great clarity, she took in the request.

"Come to me and lie against me. I would feel your essence."

Had the Stone—the immense power that sent waves of energy up to them—caught her memories with Shalt?

Go into that cavern of stormy waters? And lay exposed? She did not know this stone's energies, did not yet feel comfortable. She hadn't exactly felt comfortable with Shalt. Certainly, the first physical connections had thrown her, left her trembling and drained.

She felt the rest of the Circle waiting.

Then Mnenu's separate mind-connection touched her. "It is not dangerous. I can come with you."

"You've done this?" she asked him.

"I have."

She shivered, imagining the cold and wetness.

He chuckled in her mind. "Ash-don will warm you."

Will it help the Stone locate my daughter? She wondered. "Okay. Now?"

"Yes, I think Ash-don means now."

A narrow stairway spiraled down beneath the shelf

of stone seats. The descended it, the rungs drenched by more and more ocean until they were submerged.

And then Yanda realized what she was seeing. A glowing surface pressed up so that only the smallest edge emerged above water level. The way it curved, she knew the immensity of it. She felt Ash-don's presence pulsing through her.

# CHAPTER

# 23

**M**nenu undressed, shoving his clothes into a small compartment. They were standing on a landing a foot or more underwater.

She was reluctant, sick once again of the wetness of this life.

Mnenu stepped to her. "Remember last night when you morphed into sea creature, and the sea was warm? Can you bring back some of it?"

"Should I do that when I'm about to be against Ashdon?" Her teeth were chattering.

"All the better."

They still held the circle of minds above them. Could she transform that way?

"We can break connection from the Circle while we do this."

All at once, the connection with the others evaporated.

He stroked her back and immediately a change happened in her body. Heat built within her, or at least the feeling of cold disintegrated. She stripped and they leapt into the water.

As they approached Ash-don's surface, more adjustments occurred to her. Mnenu crawled onto the Stone, feet gripping like a newt. She followed, able to hold to the surface without any trouble.

Scintillating tremors ran along her arms at the touch to Ash-don's upper side. They reached the rounded top that stretched like a planet itself. Mnenu spread out, facedown, and she lay beside him.

A sensation surged into her, engulfing all her thoughts, and then she saw… She'd thought she had sight before, to look through walls and flesh down to the cells. Now she could view the universe. She thought of Alland and she witnessed it, as a whole planet and all its parts. She thought she'd know answers to any question. What question should she think?

I won't squander this. "Show me where Seiti is. Please."

Mnenu reached out and rested a hand on her bare shoulder. He was just one little part. of everything.

Their minds soared, scanning everywhere, sensing, feeling, sifting through minds and data, plants, animals, mountains, forests. Like a telescope one moment, and a vast siphon the next, they drew in and pulled away, close, then overarching.

Finally, all slowed. Yanda felt the stone, truly felt it. As if she could be absorbed into it. Where she ended and the stone began wasn't all that clear.

Mnenu's presence came into her awareness. Were they touching? What was touching?

Ash-don was asking her a question. It was hard to pinpoint a single thought. The thought was a being. That being was her daughter. Seiti. Her mind almost telescoped to the reality of her missing child but Ash-don pulled her back and instead of thinking, she lived her, lived their life together. Through her mind's eye, Seiti's early life paraded.

"This being is not in known space."

"What does it mean?"

"We search for unknown space."

"How?"

"Open to the Xentu in you."

Yanda's eyes popped open. "How do I do that?"

Mnenu watched her, head resting on the glowing stone, more rosy underneath them, his arms outstretched as hers were. Their fingers barely touched.

"I don't know anything about a Xentu part of me," she said. It seemed strange to speak after so much had occurred in their minds.

"Are you tired? Should we stop for now?" he asked.

"I think so." She turned her face down toward the Stone, trying to look into it, into the layers, to see the mind that pulsed with energy in its depths.

"That would be a different kind of sight, Yandawi," the Stone said to her. "We will continue in one turn."

She and Mnenu crawled until they dove into the sea, reaching the ladder and climbing. She was becoming accustomed to nakedness. It seemed somewhat external to her, both warm and dexterous in this other form.

At the lockers, she reached within her for the ability to dry, then dressed. She wore her own clothes now, what she'd brought from Alland: flexible, thermal, a style that fit her home planet. Mnenu looked her over. She was her human form again.

"Will you be attending the festivities tonight?" he asked.

"Yes." She'd forgotten this was Alyanu's last day. Tomorrow she started the long journey back to Mingal.

"You won't go, too," she'd asked Vatu, who, as far as she knew, had not returned to her home after the Fugitives escaped and completed their mission. When Yanda had raced back to Alland to be reunited with her daughter, only to find her gone.

"No. Not yet," Vatu had said, holding some secret. What was keeping her from returning home?

"Walk you to your rooms?" Mnenu asked.

"You don't have to always escort me, you know. I'm sure you have more important things awaiting your attention," Yanda said over her shoulder, as they climbed the tight spiral stairs to the Stone Circle.

Mnenu was silent and she wondered if he was hurt. She hoisted herself onto the broad stone shelf. The others were stepping off their seats, a general rumble of voices carrying through the vast chamber. Mnenu and Yanda reached the small chamber first and hung their robes. The dozen who'd recently mind-melded left together in a harmonious group, strolling along the hallways.

A Neyla male with black hair and sharp features clapped Mnenu on the back. "Quite an honor to be allowed onto Ash-don." He glanced at Yanda. "None of us ever have. What's that about?"

There was a general hush, an uncomfortable silence.

Mnenu shrugged. "Kell, if Ash-don calls…I guess we follow. You could try to go down there and see what happens." He didn't look or sound happy.

"And this one comes along. Not even Neyla. Why is she in the Circle, much less on Ash-don's surface?"

Mnenu stopped and turned to Kell, who was slightly shorter. "Yanda healed Shalt. She was the one called, of all, across the universe. I guess she has a resonance the Stones like."

The others were clustered around them, listening, looking from face to face.

A stockier Neyla gripped Kell's arm. "Come on. Let's get the party started."

Kell held back for another beat, glancing between Mnenu and Yanda, then turned to continue up the corridor, only darting one more glare behind him.

"Is there something going on with him?" Yanda asked, as they took up the tail end, letting some distance fall between them and the rest.

"He's just an ass," Mnenu said.

"You know all Neyla, right?" Yanda asked, thoughtfully.

"Yeah, I guess. We're a pretty small community."

"That would be strange, knowing people all my life. I stand out here, as a newcomer, don't I? How are strangers accepted, generally?" She hadn't even thought about it, she'd been so caught up in her own worries.

"Generally? Well, you see the visitors? We have an extensive library and appreciate the xeno-contributions."

"I see Vatu and her fellow researchers are well accepted. I guess it hadn't occurred to me that I might be resented."

They climbed the halls and tunnels, headed to Vatu's quarters on the far side of the city.

"Not all guests are included in the Circle of Ash-don," Mnenu said, giving her a quirk of a smile.

"No, I suppose not. And even with the request of a search for their daughter, not just anyone..."

"Not just anyone would be allowed into the Circle by Ash-don. The Stone wanted very much to feel your essence."

"So even if I hadn't asked…"

"Ash-don would have requested your acquaintance."

That was food for thought. "Wow."

"You remember Ash-don said he felt your shout from Alland?" Mnenu held open the door to the final hallway approaching Vatu's rooms.

"Yes. I see. You said nothing though, when I came to you, supplicant." She grinned at him. "You just liked to see me beg?"

His expression was unreadable, as though he had numerous thoughts he could express at that moment.

"Are you coming?" Vatu called into her mind.

"Yes. Almost to your door, as you probably already know." She stepped ahead of Mnenu.

Vatu opened it. She wore an amazing bodysuit shimmering with iridescent rainbow colors. "We have to get you ready for the ball. And then to the Neyna shore tomorrow for Withum." When Vatu was excited her head nubs stood on end. With all the ocean swimming and pure air, the nubs stayed now brilliant shades of jade to pale blue with a touch of gold. "Hello, Mnenu."

Yanda stepped into Vatu's room and let them greet with cheeks pressed on each side. Alyena did the same.

Mnenu looked around. "You've hung some of your Mingal sea-art here. I like it."

"Come in and look closer," she invited.

"I mustn't. Mom is having family in to start the festivities. I must make my appearance."

Did Yanda feel a twinge of disappointment at not being invited? But he'd said it was family only. Get a grip, she scolded herself.

Once he left, she turned to Alyena. "I heard this is your

last day."

"I leave tomorrow night, after the Withum ceremony. Vatu won't let me miss it."

"From the star port? Are you going on Tlalit's ship?"

"No. I'll be taking a few detours."

"Come." Vatu grabbed Yanda's hand. "We have the
perfect thing for you."

Part of Yanda wanted a little place of her own, to curl
up and think about the tremendous thing that had happened to her today. Even with the disappointment, that
Seiti may not be found—at least not by Ash-don—and
this mission might fail, she had seen and felt all the
known universe, and maybe more. She had felt herself
part of Ash-don, together with Mnenu. That had drawn
their connection closer. Now she'd transformed with him,
twice, and gone to Ash-don's depths with him.

Vatu tugged her in front of the closet.

Yanda stared at the garment Alyena displayed. It had
gradations from green-black cascading to palest jade. It
fitted from neck to ankles, yet parts flowed downward
with grace. A day ago, she would not have imagined herself in it—she went more for cargo pants and comfortable
shirts. But Yanda knew instinctively it would form to her
and flow in the waters of the sea.

"Some of us are swimming to the Neyna shore." Vatu
pulled the fantastic suit and held it against Yanda. "Put it
on, and for tonight wear this over it." She flaunted a jacket
that perfectly complemented the body suit with subtly
shimmering fabric. "And these."

The boots were sinewy. Yanda wondered if her feet
were changing permanently. They felt different, supple,
strong, aware of every surface they encountered. She
pulled off her clothes and worked the outfit on, then the

deep green footwear, with just the slightest rise at the heel which she sensed would become something else when she transformed. Last she swept on the drape, adding extra drama for the Vatu and Alyena who watched with approval.

The three made a splendid entrance into the large hall decorated for the occasion. Vaulted ceilings were lit by myriad tiny float globes that moved and swirled.

Yanda took in the scene. All the visiting scholars and most of the Neyla population were gathered in the hall.

If the Neyna's singing was ethereal, the Neyla's sounds that suddenly surrounded her, filling the vast room deep in the sea mountain, thrilled her. Vatu put her voice into it and Yanda could not resist doing the same. Every cell in her zinged with energy. And then the dancing began.

# CHAPTER

# 24

Hours later, aching, Yanda fell into bed. She hugged the pillow.

She'd barely slept when Vatu shook her, dawn light touching their quarters with a rose glow.

"No, no, you go without me," Yanda mumbled, turning away toward the wall. "I'll go on the boat."

Vatu put hands on Yanda's sides and Yanda transformed. Her cells suddenly longed to be in the water. She sat bolt upright.

"You little sea-devil." Yanda threw back the covers and scrambled out of bed.

"Wear this again." Vatu was outfitted in a suit of coruscating blue hues.

Alyena joined them, coming from the washing room. Her outfit was brilliant shades of sunset. Clearly she too had transformed for the occasion.

Yanda flashed on the fact that she had not called her son, or checked to see if Ash-don had located her daughter.

"After Withum," she thought. Then that will be all I do.

They hurried out into the hallway and raced down the long tunnel.

A connecting tube led to a shelf overlooking a breathtaking inlet. Like an atoll, palms and flowering plants surrounded jewel-like waters touched by the rising sun, and lit up. Others were gathering and they dove in, so anxious to be in the waters it was like a hunger.

A phalanx of Neyla and other transforming beings moved through the waters, graceful, sinewy, powerful. They left the inlet, entering the open seas.

Mnenu caught up with Yanda, catching her eye with a flash of a smile before he dove and then propelled out of the water, soaring upward thirty feet. He plummeted back in with hardly a splash. She was laughing when he returned to her side and slipped under her, gliding along with her until they dove and leapt together.

When she came down, Vatu shot past her, dancing on the surface of the water.

They stopped cavorting and took in the long miles with sweeping driving movements of their sinewy bodies. It was a thrill to be swimming with so many others. Yanda marveled at being in deep sea water when she'd never swum in more than a pool before this, yet another instinct altogether had taken over.

*Tesu* joined them, leaping past, diving under. Mnenu caught a dorsal fin. Many others did the same, covering great swaths of sea in only moments.

Somewhere out in the middle, with no shore in sight, nothing in any direction, a voltage shuddered through her. She paused mid-swim—had been coasting after her long legs, now forming into a tail over her feet, had pumped hard—and let the others pass her. Alone, treading water and circling, she floated, testing her senses. It came from below, this blast of energy.

Sending feelers and sight downward, she knew. It was where the two stones touched. *I have to return here after Withum*, she vowed, sure this was essential. With a powerful thrust of her tail, she darted forward to catch up with the rest.

At midday, they arrived at the shore Yanda remembered. Tall trees draped over the sand, stretching into forests and up hillsides.

Even as Yanda approached the sloping sand of the shore, her tail manifested back into feet—supple, strong feet that knew much about where they stepped. Warm and in control, confident and aware, she walked toward land, drying as she went. Her bodysuit, shades from green-black to palest lichen, fluffed out and draped gracefully. With the other Neyla, she strode up the beach toward the awaiting Neyna who circled the small inlet.

Garlands of flowers swung from tree to tree in the noonday sun. The sweet scent of Withum filled the air. They must have had their campfire the night before. Yanda remembered the amazing ceremony and felt sad to have missed it. The Neyla had started their own.

Her mind entered the meld with the thousand others. She experienced that same sweet knowing and immense love that the Withum had brought a year before.

Her eyes found Zamani, Merne, Tlalit and the other Neynas she'd been with in Shalt's Circle.

The time she'd missed didn't matter. The joining began and felt eternal.

Her hands felt suddenly warm as Mnenu took one, Vatu the other. She grinned at each of them.

Zamani's eyes watched her with intensity, even as

their minds were as one. Her memory went back to the previous year, when she'd gone to Merne's house, close by, with Tenali, and they'd spent the night together watching the dawn. Where was he?

As if in silent agreement, many lay on the sand. Yanda spooned into Mnenu, Vatu at her back. Was this to be her Neyla-Mingal Withum experience?

Those were the last of her thoughts. Her mind soared away as she returned to that place out at sea, where the Great Stones touched. Then from the surface of the sea, her spirit sank, down, down, down, 'til her feet contacted the crevice where the Stones touched. But she did not stop there. She slipped on and was within the Stones, half of her in Shalt, the other in Ash-don.

Her awareness took in the planet as a whole, the immensity of the oceans beyond their small part of the world, and then left the planet altogether.

Yanda gazed at the receding planet of Terlond and knew the two stones had been small moons. Instead of colliding, they'd been drawn to each other in a swirl of formation, and spun, remaining precisely in their perfect orbs as a new planet formed. Yanda watched this astounding occurrence as if with timelapse photography over millennia.

Then she looked outward, toward the universe. Her sight soared away, covering lightyears until she saw Tenali—saw his mind, his essence—at the end of the known cosmos. Not far from Mingal. And nowhere in that known space was her daughter.

But called.

"Seiti," she called.

Maybe all the Neyla and Neyna minds heard it because she cried out with every part of her existence. Yes, they did hear, for they called with her. The Stones as well. All called. Tenali's face turned to her, and called with them, joined their shared essence.

How long they remained, she could not know, but she felt the knowing of all as she departed from the Stones' shared edge, floated upward and away, returning to her body.

After a time, as each jointly processed what happened—the Neyna and Neyla coalescing for the first time in the unity of the two Stones that had given their Elven communities love and energy, generation upon generation and shouted out into the Unknown Universe from the edge of the Known—their awareness slowly drifted back into individual minds. Rows of gently spooned Elves, Mingal visitors, and a few other beings, moved apart, sat up on the sand, took in the surrounding sea and forest. Some lay back down, others stood, or jumped into the water. But they knew what they knew, and they were changed by it.

Yanda sat cross-legged, bowed her head, and wept. Mnenu scooted close and wrapped his arms around her. Vatu rolled so her head rested on Yanda's leg, catching Yanda's tears on her face, doing nothing about them. Yanda rested a hand on Vatu's nubs, and laid her head on Mnenu's shoulder.

Zamani, Merne, and Tlalit came and sat near them, knees touching her, each other. Yanda's eyes locked with Zamani's.

They shared the vision of Tenali—Zamani's grandson, Merne's son—out there at the edge of the known universe, considering leaving it to go into the Unknown.

The six again shared minds in a small Circle. They felt others join to help as they sent their thoughts to Tenali.

"Wait, son," Merne said to him.

Tenali looked up, feeling their presence again.

"Yanda?" He breathed the word, using not just his mind but his voice.

She loved hearing him.

He seemed to become aware of Mnenu pressed close to her and held back whatever he was going to say next. "I've followed sightings of your daughter as far as I could."

"I didn't know that's why you left Alland," she said, self-conscious that so many other minds heard them.

"I'm sorry I didn't tell you."

Okay, this needed to get less personal. "I think I could go into the Stones again and maybe reach farther. Are you in a place where you can wait a bit?"

"Yeah. I can. I have a few paid deliveries to make along the Edge. I'll hang around here."

"Thank you. For trying and...for waiting."

They broke the connection as Neyna and Neyla emerged from the trees carrying platters of food.

Yanda felt drained, but alive. That's what Withum did.

A large tray set between them contained heaps of fruits, mushroom cheeses, sweet spiced *patas*, and flat breads for dipping. Summer wine sparkled in slender jugs and tall glasses.

Though difficult to pull her mind away from the recent revelations—particularly the gone-ness of her daughter, just reinforced—Yanda allowed herself to drift into casual conversation.

Mnenu got up to speak with someone, and Zamani stepped closer. "I can have Zami brought here to you," he said.

"It's alright. I'll return home to him soon."

"Home?" He was clearly struggling to be pleasant. "Yanda." He lowered his voice to almost a whisper. "You and Zami have a home here, always. Now that you know where your daughter is, you have no need to return to the Outback of Alland. Is that not correct?"

"Who says I don't intend to return to my surgery practice in Skarth?" She couldn't help getting her back up. It always felt wrong to speak this way with the reserved, generous Elven leader, yet that made her even angrier.

"Once you've found your daughter, I'm sure that could happen. Or you could help build a surgery here, in Dondar. Would that be so bad?"

He made her feel so unreasonable. It was a tempting idea. A practice where she did not need to hide her abilities, could use them openly and keep learning more? But the more he pushed, the more she resented it. What would be so wrong with bringing Zami here, to know his Elven folk? She'd always planned to return for visits with him. But to build all her hopes and plans around Dondar where she'd remained captive for so long?

"I understand your hesitation," he said, gently.

That was when she hated mind-reading. And he could do it so easily, without her knowing he was there. Not with evil intent, as Krid had. Only to better care for those he loved. But where do caring and controlling overlap and become one?

Vatu put a delicate hand on Yanda's leg. Quietly, eyes shining, she said, "We were just on the Edge, near my home."

"*Arspat tinas kahay*," Zamani said gently, and asked into Yanda's mind, "Can we walk?"

Yanda shook her head, all but glaring at Zamani. She

squeezed Vatu's hand. "I know. How did that feel?"

"Good. You need to go there, don't you?"

Yanda stared at her. Vatu had hoped to show Yanda her home but it was so very far away. "Unless Tenali finds her and brings her back."

"Do you think he can find her without you?"

Go into the Unknown universe. Would her special sight do her any good there?

Zamani stood and walked away.

# CHAPTER

# 25

Yanda watched Zamani's tall stately figure a moment, then said to Vatu, "I'd love to accompany you home. I'd bring Zami."

Mnenu had returned and settled by them again. Yanda turned to him. "Maybe you could teach my son to transform to sea-elf."

"Most likely. He's part Xentu, too."

"And half Neyna."

Vatu's nubs stood on end, a brilliant cerulean shade of blue. "You must."

"So much to contemplate." Yanda wanted to continue the battle to bring her home planet toward accepting magical abilities. But it wasn't the only place in the universe that needed help. What about those enslaved on Blaz? Or the criminals tied to Krid? He needed to be stopped from stealing power objects from around the universe, and especially from abducting magical beings.

Zamani stood again nearby. "Will you at least spend

the night? We can call the Circle together."

Yanda glanced at Mnenu. "The Neyla return to Zotoul?"

"Soon," he responded, also in mind-speak, to her only.

"I'll return with the Neyla," she said to Zamani. "But I'll bring Zami to visit you soon."

Zamani turned abruptly and walked into the forest.

"Whoops. I think you ticked off the leader of the Neyna," Mnenu said. "Brave."

"Why brave?" she asked.

"Most wouldn't."

She pondered that.

"You look stunning, by the way. I can see why he doesn't want you to leave."

She flicked sand onto him, though she grinned at his compliment. Then sobered. "He wants Zami."

"He wants you and Zami. Who wouldn't?" He watched her with serious eyes, though a smile played around his lips.

She swung to face him. "I'm kind of a lot of trouble, actually."

"I'll say." He flicked sand in his turn.

"Let's swim," Vatu said, never tiring of the sea, her natural habitat.

"Has Alyena left?"

Vatu nodded, eyes tearing up.

* * *

On the swim back, again getting help from the *tesu*, they made strong progress, Withum giving them sustained energy, and the connection of minds still shared. As far as she could see were leaping forms, catching the glowing orange light as sunset approached.

Yanda sensed when the place where the Stones touched grew near. In fact, it drew her. But not now; it had been enough for one day to have been within them, seen so much of the universe. She sent a mental promise to return soon. The sea rumbled beneath her and she laughed, spun in the water, dove and shot upward, arcing, sliding back in. The Neyla and visitors played the rest of the way back.

It was high tide and Yanda saw only a few rock spires indicating the location of the underwater city. She imagined light cascading through the towers, into the halls.

Vatu swam with friends.

Mnenu took Yanda's hand and pulled her toward an underwater entrance. They dove beneath a stone arch and down a narrow channel, arriving in a deep pool. Mnenu shot from the water, landing on a ledge and held out his hand, inviting her to do the same. She climbed steps instead, though she could have vaulted up.

Mnenu said, "This is near my quarters. Will you come with me there now?"

"No responsibilities to attend to?" she asked, one brow quirked up.

"Nothing goes on after Withum," he said.

They walked hand in hand, drying as they went.

Several stairways and hallways took them to Mnenu's rooms. The panel slid open at his touch, and closed after them. He slipped his arms around her and enticed her into a long kiss.

For the first time, they made love in a bed. It was sweet and unhurried, made more amazing by the recent mind-share that seemed to have expanded all senses.

After, Mnenu brought her hot chocolate, and a small handheld device. She ran her fingers over it, taking in the quality of the fine, slender molding. "From Dorn?" she asked.

He nodded. "You can call your son on it." He touched the side, and a miniscule screen lit up. "I'm going to do work in my office. You remember how to retrieve Andle's code?"

She searched in her mind, found the chest of drawers, one marked "code", and nodded, pleased with herself.

He selected a program, showing her its symbol, then left the room, closing the door.

She put in the numbers. Zami's face appeared. Did he look older? She gripped the device, examining him. In turn, he pressed against the screen on his end, putting his little lips to the surface. She kissed him back, then sang him a bedtime song; it seemed to be night there. He put his tiny chin on his hand and listened.

"Tell me what you've been doing," she said.

He rattled off some activities, including a few worrying moves. "When are you coming, Mama?"

"Soon. I'll be there before you know it."

"How can you do that?" he asked.

"You'll see," she said, stomach jerking with a laugh at his literal mind, believing anything possible, capable of much. "Kiss the animals for me and take good care of them, and Andle."

"I will. We might have to move again. Will you find us?"

"Always, Button. Can you put Andle on?"

When her Allandian friend appeared, she asked for a rundown, and Andle gave it.

"I won't ask for a location. I'll connect minds with you when we near Alland."

"Does this mean you found your daughter?" Andle asked.

"No. Sort of. I know more than I did. I think."

Andle didn't ask for any more detail. She put Zami back on. Yanda reclined against the pillows. This time they had leisure for some of their favorite jokes and word games. Yanda could tell this little device had max encryption.

Too soon, though, they had to part. "I'm coming," she assured her son.

After, she lay thinking, aching to hold her boy in her arms.

When Mnenu returned, Yanda lay on her side, cradling the little Dorn device like a baby bird in her two hands. She sat up. "I have to go back into the Stones. I think I should go to where they meet."

Mnenu sat on the bed. "We can bring the boat."

The second time making love in his room was better. Spending all night together was best of all. Well, right up there.

\* \* \*

At breakfast, Yanda arrived with Mnenu, wearing her outfit from the day before. Vatu, sitting with other Mingalians and an eclectic array of beings, waved.

Mnenu glanced around and quickly kissed her cheek, then made a small plate of food and headed to his office.

Yanda joined Vatu, studying the group as she ate; one had barnacles, others were smooth, a few undulated like seaweed in water, eyes set to the sides of narrow heads, mere extensions of their necks. Most used mind-speak since the sounds made were impossible to translate comprehensibly.

Vatu drank down the last of her *kran* as Yanda tried out new caviars and chutneys with morning sweet-spiced flat breads.

"I want to take you to caverns and tidepools on the east side. Are you ready?" Vatu asked.

"Am I!" Yanda said, with her new avid taste for all things *sea*.

Vatu took her to crystal caves cascading with coruscating light. They'd changed in Vatu's quarters. Yanda wore a lavender bodysuit, Vatu a medley of hues that seemed to pick up the cavern's hues like a chameleon. Maybe she did.

Yanda felt Mnenu's mind. She shot him a picture of her and Vatu in the crystal caves.

"Can I join you?" Mnenu asked.

"Of course," she answered.

With her new sea-sense, Yanda knew depths and distances. Smell, which was really taste, told her about tides, weather, and nearby creatures. Wither her heightened sight, she spotted Mnenu entering the pools from the dark tunnel.

In no time at all, he rocketed out of the water near them, sleek in a chocolate and sun-yellow suit.

They left the pools, gliding as one through channels, like a pod of *tesu*, their hearts palpitating in unison, and she grinned at the sheer pleasure of sharing this.

They emerged on the far side of the mountain from the city, in a playland cove. Cliffs offered holes to climb in, and chutes to slide out, scattering phosphorescence.

As the tide lowered, they climbed to a flat, sunny rock and lay talking, enjoying the warmth.

Suddenly Yanda felt the immense throb of Ash-don calling vibrating through her bones. "I think I have to go."

Being the Stone's Voice, Mnenu heard as well and stood.

They hugged Vatu and left through a different channel to arrive at Tsatari, Ash-don's cave with the Circle's stone seats. Without checking whether anyone sat in the Circle, or even if he followed, Yanda descended the ladder to the lower shelf and dropped into the water. This time she crossed to the Stone with long, sure strokes, and disappeared inside.

Was she spirit-being or still her physical self? She could not tell. It was as though she was made of the same substance as the stone, yet could move through. She was drawn instantly to the juncture of the two Stones.

Floating in a timeless state, she saw outward to the stars and past them. She felt herself there in space, a part of it, and knew when she was beyond the Known Universe. There was an Otherness in the dark matter there.

And she saw her daughter. Older than when she'd last seen her, of course, but older than she would be now. *Am I seeing the future? Or dreaming?* Yanda couldn't tell. Seiti—beautiful Seiti—her long, wild, dark hair, with crimson streaks like her mother's, set off by black tones underneath. They'd always been that way. She looked like a teen, but poised, powerful beyond any age.

A breeze carried bits of fluff in the air. Was it flower pods? They caught refracted rainbows that came from nowhere and everywhere. What was this place? Seiti slowly turned, arms out, increasing speed, whirling. It seemed ecstatic, yet her daughter did not laugh, did not smile. She seemed to concentrate. Purposefully, Yanda looked around, taking in the strange landscape, gray-blue, with extraordinary hill formations, odd torpedo-shaped clouds—or were they ships—but her eyes returned quickly to her daughter. She dropped to her knees, arms outstretched and Seiti ran to her.

Was she holding her? Seiti felt solid. Yanda pushed back to study her daughter's face. Sobs rose. Hiccupped laughs and tears mingled as their cheeks pressed together. But Seiti'd changed. Yanda stared into her daughter's eyes and slipped into fathomless depths. Someone had taught her to hide thoughts and memories. Or maybe she'd discovered the ability herself.

"I don't know how long I have," Yanda said, or thought she said it. "We must share our stories. Will you tell me yours?"

"Not now," came the answering thought from her daughter.

Yanda realized Seiti hadn't yet spoken a word. "Who's caring for you?" Yanda asked, looking around for any sign of habitat and seeing none. "Where are you staying?"

Seiti thought into her mind, "Can you take me with you?"

Yanda suppressed a heartbroken cry. "I'm here only in spirit, darling. I have to figure out where you are, and come get you."

All too human panic surged in Yanda. She tried to hold onto her daughter but she'd spoken the words, "only in spirit", and like a spell breaking, it all vanished. She was pushed from the Stone, crawling like a salamander down its side.

# CHAPTER

# 26

**M**nenu approached through the water. Yanda caught his thoughts, about her "fabulous *lanten* shape". She saw through his eyes her shoulders slightly brawnier, tail-fin covered in smooth iridescent scales before they split into legs and she crawled down Ash-don's side to him. As she slipped into the sea, her legs again felt boneless, undulating, holding her in place.

Vatu cruised toward them. Coming up beside Yanda, she studied her face. "Are you alright?" she asked in mind-speak.

"What made you come here?" Yanda inquired, darting a worried glance toward Ash-don. Would it hurt Vatu to be so close?

"Your mind disappeared," Vatu said, placing her hand against the Stone.

Yanda and Mnenu stared.

Ash-don rumbled, "Stop worrying. I like the Mingal."

Yanda slapped her hand to her mouth as mirth bubbled up.

"Want to go? Or stay?" Vatu asked.

Yanda saw laughter percolating in Mnenu's eyes as well; they pushed off. They'd worried for nothing.

"I think Ash-don has had enough of me," Yanda said, her voice shaking with unreleased laughter.

"Never," came the Stone's objection.

Mnenu climbed the ladder first and offered a hand to the other two.

Yanda was glad Ash-don knew Vatu, too. It was one more thing they shared.

Vatu glanced back at her and Yanda caught the Mingal's thought: Friend, soul mate. I'm glad, too.

Yanda knew some of Vatu's fondness came from the months when she'd taken care of her, clearing the suffocating congestion from her lungs in toxic Dondar. But it wasn't just gratitude.

As Yanda said goodbye to Ash-don, the Stone answered, "That place. New place. But familiar. Maybe."

A sliver of hope renewed itself in the midst of her tragic emotions, not being able to bring Seiti with her. "She wanted to come," Yanda thought, and she held onto this.

The Stone had a way of closing connection. This time, however, there was a difference. Ash-don had reached for her, needed her.

As the three walked through the round room where the robes hung, unused this time, Vatu asked if Yanda had found anything.

Yanda told her about Unknown Space.

To their amazement, her friend said, "I've been there before, but only in spirit travel. In my planet's trainings, we often spirit-traveled among the stars." She knew the Otherness of Dark Matter outside Known Space. She'd feared Yanda's spirit might never return from it. "If you were an average being, it might not have."

Mnenu was staring at Yanda and she mouthed, "Don't say it," knowing Xentu would be the next topic.

He shook his head, giving her the look. "You'll have to come to terms with your blood someday," but he only bowed and turned down the hall that passed his office. "I should do a few things. Want to get lunch in a bit?"

They agreed.

At his doorway, he shot a mind-message, "The Sea Horse."

Vatu knew the one he meant. They grabbed devices from her rooms and went ahead to the restaurant.

Their suits had fluffed into presentable attire. Yanda was no longer minding a slight sea-salt coating. Or maybe her skin absorbed it better now. She checked her arms to see as they crossed the café. Pretty smooth!

Situated on a promontory, this hall allowed a view of splashing waves through spangled windows. Blue-black walls glistened like obsidian. Admiring the contrast with beams of light cast from the tall windows, Yanda realized Mnenu was signaling to them from the level above.

"How'd you get here first?" She laughed, climbing the curving stairs.

"Couldn't concentrate," he said.

Yanda saw the gleam in his eyes. He'd told her everything felt new, exciting, unexpected since she'd dropped into their lives. She saw near panic as she caught his thought, that she might soon disappear. She rested a hand on his arm as she scooted into the booth next to him and turned to Vatu.

"Anything here remind you of Mingal?" Yanda asked playfully, not imagining Vatu had a seahorse café on her planet.

Vatu's eyes glowed as she looked around. "In ways. I think I need to tell my people about some of these design ideas, though." A wave crashed onto the balcony below, allowing water to cross the sill. "When I was in this dining hall before, it was a gray day so I didn't get the full impact."

Facing them, Vatu picked up a seaweed-and-salt shaker, sprinkled some delicately into her palm and licked, eyes crinkling semi-apology. "I'm so rude, but yum."

A *vandamar* approached with a large tray.

"I took the liberty of choosing some items already," Mnenu said.

Yanda's eyes widened when the waiter handed her a plate with a steaming hot pocket.

Mnenu reached and pressed a pad the waiter held out. Figures lit up on the surface. "Thank you, Crick," Mnenu said.

The sea-horse-like fellow bowed. Yanda thought she may have detected a sort of smile from the wide mouth. He dropped to all fours and trotted away, tail curling and uncurling behind him. She'd tried to read if there were any mind signal. There had been a vague chitter but no discernable ideas that she could catch, or she couldn't recognize their pattern.

Plates made of shells offered bright dips.

Yanda broke open her pastry. "Yum." Sauce made of sea vegetables and mushrooms gave off a rich aroma. "What's in this?" she asked. "Something I can't identify."

Mnenu gave her a mind-picture of a sea flower. "*Dolu*."

"Ah." She nibbled, then dipped a wafer-thin cracker into one of the sauces.

They tried everything he'd ordered. Hunger satisfied, Yanda sat back and grew silent.

Mnenu glanced at Vatu who returned his gaze and scrunched her face.

"Stop mind-gossiping, you two. I might be a tad morose but I can still talk." Yanda curled a leg so her knee nudged Mnenu's side, and let her head fall against the back of the bench.

Mnenu stroked her hand. "I'm sorry. I was trying to be…delicate."

"I held my daughter. Or it seemed like her, but she wasn't eight. Older. So maybe it was in the future. I don't know where she is, or how to get to her. But Ash-don…"

"Yeah, maybe in the process, Ash-don will find his sister moon." Mnenu took a bite of Yanda's mushroom pastry.

She played with crackers, lining them around her plate. Thoughtfully, she said, "Why would Seiti end up on their sister moon, though? What are the chances of that?"

"Well, we're sure as hell gonna find out." Tlalit walked toward them, holding Zami, and dropped into the seat next to Vatu.

Yanda stared, rising from her seat, arms outstretched for her little boy.

After some laughing and crying, with Yanda feeling Zami up and down to make sure he was really there, she said, "I don't get it. I've been on Terlond less than a week. How could you get to Alland and back to bring Zami? I mean, that was you on the ship with me, wasn't it, coming to Terlond? Or was it a…clone?" She kissed Zami's cheek.

He was on his knees peering into her face, lower lip trembling.

"You know Merne has special...ways, Yanda," Tlalit said.

"Oh, special *ways*, is it?" Merne stood at the top of the stairs. She was moving slowly. She packed into their too-full booth, squeezing next to Tlalit. "I learned some things from Shouma. I can bounce. Across space."

"Makes my ship pretty superfluous." Tlalit snagged a fried *sadi snip* from Mnenu's plate.

Yanda bounced forward. "You did that with Zami?" She sat back, too happy to have her son with her to protest too long, and mumbled, "It better not have been your first experiment."

Merne rose up enough to catch the waiter's eye on the level below, and gestured, then sat. "We were in Rotoul. Then we were on Alland. And back again. All in a flash. He helped, actually."

"That's baby-napping." Yanda grumbled.

"I wanted to surprise you. I could tell where things were going."

"What the *beezus* does that mean?" Grateful as she was, Yanda felt cornered. If Merne would take this kind of decision on herself, what else would she do?

"Oh, come on." Merne slumped back in the seat. "At Withum, we went to the place where the Stones touch with you, saw you go into Unknown Space. We later saw you go to your daughter on that weird moon."

"You saw? I thought...thought it might have just been a vision." Yanda's cheeks warmed and tears threatened.

Merne rested her powerful, swirling, gold-centered eyes on Yanda. "I don't think so, Yawi."

# EPILOGUE

**Mnenu**

To tell the truth, I didn't think she'd let me come. We're packing. Vatu's already taken loads to the Sarsefi, which is floating out on the water. She has books and souvenirs from her time with us, and her college stuff.

I don't know what to bring. Yanda says she has nothing. Tlalit says we'll have everything we need on board. And that we can stop in worlds along the way.

Tenali's out there, waiting. For her? Who knows. The guy's not steady. Who can trust him? Yanda shouldn't. He abducted her for Krid, for shell's sake.

Zami's a great kid. Man, those eyes. Part Yanda, part Neyna. He already has a lot of powers. And loving. He's a loving little guy.

I never thought I'd see Mingal, much less leave Known Space. If we even figure out where we're going. I don't care. I just want to be part of it.

# THE END

Watch for Book 3 in the series,
*Missing Moon of the Xentu*

COMING SOON!

# A FAR CRY GLOSSARY

**Abdil:** one of the fellow doctors Yanda had trusted.

**Alland:** terra-formed planet where Yanda grew up; no tall trees or mountains, no oceans

**Alyena:** Mingal scholar, Vatu's friend, visiting the Neyla.

**Ambas:** a saying, maybe an ancient god from an old belief.

**Andle:** rebel – female. Rescues wounded animals.

**Aradon:** Qontaqian; strong enough to subdue Jelat.

*arash:* a plant-based milk from an Allandian grain but a hybrid from several planets' genuses to suit the climate.

**Arc:** man of strong mind powers; centuries-old; keeper of Pedore.

**Ash-don:** Elf Stone of the Neyla.

**Aspar:** bright crimson Terlondian fruit.

*Balyou:* the small town on Alland where Yanda grew up.

**Beril:** young Pedorean, does childcare and other chores.

**Blaz:** planet known for trafficking, violence, slavery.

**Blenin:** city on Shagal, where Seiti may have been spotted.

**Button:** Yanda's nickname for her son, Zami.

**buzz pen:** a decryptor.

**Canda:** woman on the farm, shelter to refuges.

*Catatuga:* like a carrot.

**Cellin:** powerful woman who seems to run Pedore.

**chaka:** like hot chocolate.

*chepootle*: a sticky bun with sweet spices and apricot layered in.

**Church of Vital Promise:** powerful single main church of **Alland;** has grown xenophobic; intimately tied with government.

**Cillen:** powerful woman who seems to run Pedore, Keeper.

**Citadel:** Krid's mansion in Dondar; prison for fems with powers.

**cockleberry:** orange fruit

**Colo:** little girl, Merem's daughter, at Pedore.

*Cuffa*: coffee of Alland.

**Da-Lam:** program allowing encrypted searches.

**Dalaton:** Merem's tiny town.

**Dalatonean:** encompasses the small settlements of Cillen and Soni.

*dali frond*: like chard.

*decryptor*: reads encrypted text, decoding.

*dolu*: sea flower.

*Dundri*: thin plaz blinds remotely controlled, suspended in air against transparent plaz windows.

**Dondar:** main city on Terlond's single continent.

**Dorn:** planet known for high quality, especially innovative high-end tech.

**duddle-nuts:** toasted spiced Allandian nuts like pistachios

**ENAC 370:** high end device

**entati:** rebel wanderer

**exo-signs:** marks of unusual origin.

**fajan:** lover, partner.

**Farn:** moon where Yanda was first imprisoned by Kridenit.

**fems:** females of humanoid species

*Fiti*: communication device on Alland.

*floofle bennie*: a filled puffy pastry.

*froshers*: analyze for disease at space port and entry points.

**gallihoe:** like a bus; powered by magnetic fields.

**grest:** cash on Alland.

**hajar:** green fruit like plums.

**Ilan:** big red-haired man; can shield powerfully; from Qontaq. Part of the Alland underground.

**Jelat:** one of the Keepers of Pedore; travels to Skarth often; tech whiz.

**Kalden:** male Neyla, techie

**Keelit:** Qontaqian; Ilan's associate.

**Kelef:** rebel friend – male.

**Kell:** Neyla female, pinched features black hair, jealous over/of Mnenu.

**Kishan:** female matrix worker; met in Yanda's apartment.

**Kodok:** spice on Alland.

**Kridenit "Krid":** evil mage; collects objects and creatures with powers.

**kran:** coffee of the Neyla.

**Lalut:** prism-shaped electronic device.

**lanten:** sea form, for Elves

**Lark:** Tenali's ship.

**Lassa:** means young mother in Dalatonean.

**Lo'l's Place:** a café bakery in Balyou.

**Malu:** female Neyla who came for Yanda when she first landed in their waters.

**meezy:** term of endearment in Cillen's native language.

**Merem:** mother of a toddler Colo in Pedore.

**Merne:** leader of the Neyna elves, Zamani's daughter, hair brown and green; can transform herself into other shapes.

**Mingalean:** from Mingal, a far planet at the edge of the known universe, all ocean.

**Mnenu:** male sea elf.

*Muldoo sprouts:* veg like brussel sprouts.

*nagal:* meaning fantastic in Mingalean.

**Nedri:** Yanda's adoptive father from infancy.

**Neyla:** sea elves on planet Terlond

**Nic-nic:** marsupial, with Andle.

**Ollie:** an underground tech rebel in Skarth.

**Omshi:** Yanda's adoptive mother from infancy

**Outer Alland:** where rebels are hidden.

**Pedore:** secret underground facility by Church of the Vital Promise.

**Plaz:** synthetic material made from recyclables or plant fibers; can be thin as paper or thicker, molded into shapes like plastic.

*ploto:* tall Allandian bird that lays large eggs in marshlands.

**plunka-toys:** plaz pieces fit together to build elaborate structures.

**Rari eggs:**

**Rotoul:** Elven forest on Terlond.

**Rotoulian:** of Rotoul.

**Sabra:** gnomish Qontaqian.

*sadi snips:* root vegetable like parsnip.

**sala:** poultry eggs.

**Sandor:** rebel friend, male

**Sarsefi:** lovemaking, also Tlalit's ship name.

**Satarn:** crater with gardens next to Pedore.

**Satiyati:** sweet satiyati is used in baking, like nutmeg.

*Sawa ninga:* greeting in a language both Cillen and Soni speak.

*scanda:* worn out, tired in Allandian

**Sedon:** Qontaqian associated with Ilan.

*sedpods:* single- or two-passenger bikes, some covered.

**Seiti:** Yanda's \daughter, 8 years old.

**Sentori Sector:** where Takmik is from.

**Setoin:** a rebel in the outback.

**Shagal:** moon where Seiti might have been caught on camera monitor.

**Shalt:** immense power stone of the Neyna.

**Shatari:** a game with picture cards.

**Sheffed:** rough borough of Dondar.

*shilf:* hand held device at Pedore.

*Shouma:* woman with formidable mind powers, captive with Yanda, trained the fems.

*sidu:* Elven incense.

**Sinisay:** that part of the government that monitored talent, prevented its use, sequestered its powers.

**Skarth:** main city on Alland, where Yanda was surgeon; large spaceport.

**Soni:** a Keeper of Pedore; Healer.

*Sutati:* rebel gathering before breaking camp.

*Swizzer:* a sled that floats using a magnetic field, used especially in caves.

**synth-sara-skin:** Allandian carnivore, now extinct.

**Takmik:** sentient sea creature visiting the Neyla. Dome-headed, with pointy teeth — was it a he? Robed with a high collar, stately; eyes close set but bulbous, nose holes like a pair of sea caves.

**Tenali:** half-elf grandson son of Neyna leader, Zamani

**Tellot:** (Gisli) planet of fragile, semi-tropical climate and nonviolent culture.

**Terlond:** planet of Yanda's captivity; where the woodland and sea elves live. Mostly ocean.

*tesu*: dolphin like, on Terlond.

**tika:** like sesame.

**Tlalit:** Merne's love, now ship captain.

**Tokong:** rabbit in Qontaqian.

**Tsatari:** ancient sacred name of the mountain, as well as the knowing that came only in this place of Ash-don.

vandamar: waiter.

**Vashal:** in the Elven forest; where the Crystal Pyramid houses the Circle of Elves trained to hold up the invisible protective dome.

**Vatu:** Yanda's friend, fellow fugitive from Krid; home planet Mingal, all water.

**weejon:** eel-like

**Withum:** flower whose pollen brings on a great mind-meld among the Elves one day a year.

**woo-loo:** tiny marsupial creature of Outer Alland.

**Xentu:** powerful, long-living people who have been missing from the known universe for some time.

**Yanda:** main character.

**Yandawi:** Yanda's Xentu name

**Zamani:** leader of the forest elves on Terlond.

**Zami:** Yanda and Zamani's son.

**Za-Za:** nickname for Zami.

**Zebel:** rebel friend of Setoin.

**Zotoul:** Neyla realm, including reefs and waters

# LIST OF ALL THE PLANETS
# GROUPED IN STAR SYSTEMS

**Star system: Berson Sector**

Alland (Yanda)

Shagal (wild trader city Blenin where Seiti was spotted)

**Star system: Aband Sector**

Terlond

Farn -moon of neighboring planet, captivity, no air

**Star system: Craspel Sector**

Romden (Beri)

Dorn: planet known for high quality, innovative tech, often elegant in style.

Tellot: (Gisli) delicate tropical planet

**Star system: Sentori Sector**

Blaz

Elznap: (Shouma, of the Sonda culture)

Ontil: (waterworld with farout sea creatures, many very intelligent such as Takmik)

**Star system: Merdon Sector**

Qontaq (Bonden, Dele) has martial element; also spiritual opposed to war

Sandu: planet with large freighter system

Erzon (planet of the Jejod; has Prokit's Moon)

**Star system: Telori Sector**

**(farthest out in the Known Universe)**

Mingal

*Marie Judson* is an avid fantasy and sci-fi reader. She's been an editor, coffee roaster, and college professor. She lives on the wild coast of Northern California.

Visit her blog and sign up for her newsletter:
**www.mariejudson.com**